THE
WEDDING PLANNER
AND THE CEO

THE
WEDDING PLANNER
AND THE CEO

BY

ALISON ROBERTS

MILLS
BOON®

First published in Great Britain 2015
by Mills & Boon, an imprint of Harlequin (UK) Limited,
Large Print edition 2015
Eton House, 18-24 Paradise Road,
Richmond, Surrey, TW9 1SR

© 2015 Alison Roberts

ISBN: 978-0-263-25679-6

Harlequin (UK) Limited's policy is to use papers that are natural, renewable and recyclable products and made from wood grown in sustainable forests. The logging and manufacturing processes conform to the legal environmental regulations of the country of origin.

Printed and bound in Great Britain
by CPI Antony Rowe, Chippenham, Wiltshire

CHAPTER ONE

'*No?*'

The smile was sympathetic but the head-shake emphasised the negative response and the receptionist's raised eyebrows suggested that Penelope must have known she was dreaming when she thought her request might be considered reasonable.

'There must be *someone* I could speak to?' It was harder to say no face to face than over the phone, which was, after all, why she'd taken time out of her crazy schedule to fight London traffic and come to the company's head office in person.

In desperation?

'There's really no point.' The receptionist's smile faded slightly. 'You might be able to engage a cowboy to let off a few fireworks on a week's notice but to get the kind of show the best company in the country has to offer, you have to book in advance. *Months* in advance.'

'I didn't have months. My bride only decided she wanted fireworks this morning. I'm talking Bridezilla, here, you know?'

There was a wary edge to the receptionist's gaze now. Was she worried that Penelope might be capable of following her client's example and throwing an epic tantrum?

'I understand completely but I'm sorry, there's still nothing I can do to help. For future reference, you can book online to make an appointment to talk to one of our sales reps.'

'I don't want to talk to a sales rep.' Penelope tapped into the extra height her four-inch heels provided. 'I want to talk to your manager. Or director. Or whoever it is that runs this company.'

The smile vanished completely. 'We have a chief executive officer. All Light on the Night is an international company. An *enormous* international company. We do shows like the Fourth of

July on the Brooklyn Bridge in New York. New Year's Eve on the Sydney Harbour Bridge in Australia.' Her tone revealed just how far out of line Penelope had stepped. 'You might very well want to talk to him but there's no way on earth Ralph Edwards would be interested in talking to *you*.'

'Really? Why not?'

The curiosity sounded genuine and it came from a male voice behind Penelope. The effect on the young woman in front of her was astonishing. The receptionist paled visibly and her mouth opened and closed more than once, as if she was trying to recall all the vehement words that had just escaped.

Penelope turned to see a tall man and registered dark hair long enough to look tousled, faded denim jeans and…cowboy boots? One of the sales reps, perhaps?

'She…doesn't have an appointment.' The receptionist was clearly rattled. 'She just walked in and wants to book a show. A *wedding…*'

The man's gaze shifted to Penelope and made

her want to smooth the close fit of her skirt over her hips even though she knew perfectly well it couldn't be creased. Or raise a hand to make sure no errant tresses had escaped the French braiding that described a perfect crescent from one side of her forehead to meet the main braid on the back of her head.

'Congratulations.' His voice had a rich, low timbre. It made Penelope think of gravel rolling around in something thick and delicious. Like chocolate.

'Sorry?' Was he congratulating her on her choice of this company?

'On your engagement.'

'Oh…it's not *my* wedding.'

That was a dream too distant to be visible even with a telescope at the moment. And there was no point even picking up a telescope until she knew what it was she was looking for, and how could she know that until she discovered who she really was and what she was capable of? Come to think of it, this was the first step towards that distant dream, wasn't it? The first time she was taking a leap out of any known comfort zone. Doing something *she* wanted—just for herself.

'I'm an event manager,' she said, after the barely perceptible pause. 'It's my client who's getting married.'

'Ah…' The spark of polite interest was fading rapidly. 'You've come to the right place, then. I'm sure Melissa will be able to help you with whatever arrangements you want to make.'

Melissa made a choked sound. 'She wants the show next Saturday, Mr Edwards.'

Mr Edwards? The terribly important CEO of this huge international company wore faded jeans and cowboy boots to work? Penelope was clearly overdressed but she couldn't let it faze her enough to lose this unexpected opportunity.

One that was about to slip away. She saw the look that implied complete understanding and went as far as forgiving the company receptionist for her unprofessional exchange with a potential client. She also saw the body language that suggested this CEO was about to retreat to whatever top-floor executive sanctuary he'd unexpectedly appeared from.

'I'll give her a list of other companies that might be able to help,' Melissa said.

'I don't want another company.' The words burst out with a speed and emphasis that took Penelope by surprise. 'I…I have to have the best and…and you're the best, aren't you?'

Of course they were. The entire wall behind the receptionist's desk was a night sky panorama of exploding fireworks. Pyrotechnic art with a combination of shape and colour that was mind-blowing.

The man's mouth twitched. Maybe he'd been surprised, too. 'We certainly are.' Amusement reached his eyes with a glint. Very dark eyes, Penelope noticed. As black as sin, even. Her pulse skipped and sped up. There was only one thing to do when you found yourself so far out of your depth like this. Aim for the surface and kick hard.

'It might be worth your while to consider it.' She snatched a new gulp of air. 'This is a celebrity wedding. The kind of publicity that can't be bought.' She managed a smile. 'I understand you specialise in huge shows but New Year's Eve and the Fourth of July only happen once a year, don't they? You must need the smaller stuff as well? This could be a win-win situation for both of us.'

An eyebrow quirked this time. Was he intrigued by her audacity? Was that a sigh coming from Melissa's direction?

'You have a managerial board meeting in fifteen minutes, Mr Edwards.'

'Give me ten,' Penelope heard herself saying, her gaze still fixed on him. 'Please?'

She looked like some kind of princess. Power-dressed and perfectly groomed. The spiky heels of her shoes looked like they could double as a lethal weapon and he could imagine that the elegant, leather briefcase she carried might be full of lengthy checklists and legally binding contracts.

She was the epitome of everything Rafe avoided like the plague so why on earth was he ushering her into his office and closing the door behind them? Perhaps he was trying to send a message to the junior staff that even difficult clients needed to be treated with respect. Or maybe there had been something in the way she'd looked when he'd suggested it was her own wedding she'd come here to organise.

A flicker of…astonishment? He'd probably have the same reaction if someone suggested he was about to walk down the aisle.

Maybe not for the same reasons, though. The kind of people he had in his life were as non-con-formist as he was, whereas this woman looked like she'd already have the preferred names picked out for the two perfectly behaved chil-dren she would eventually produce. One girl and one boy, of course. She might have them already, tidied away in the care of a nanny somewhere, but a quick glance at her left hand as she walked past him revealed an absence of any rings so maybe it had been embarrassment that it was taking so long rather than astonishment that had registered in that look.

No. More likely it was something about the way she'd said 'please'. That icy self-control with which she held herself had jarred on both occasions with something he'd seen flicker in her face but the flicker that had come with that 'please' had looked like determination born of desperation and he could respect that kind of motivation.

'Take a seat.' He gestured towards an area that had comfortable seating around a low coffee table—an informal meeting space that had a wall of glass on one side to show off the fabulous view of the Wimbledon golf course.

Not that she noticed the gesture. Clearly impressed to the point of being speechless, she was staring at the central feature of the penthouse office. A mirror-like tube of polished steel that was broken in the middle. The layer of stones on the top of the bottom section had flames flickering in a perfect circle.

He liked it that she was so impressed. He'd designed this feature himself and he was proud of it. But he didn't have time for distractions like showing off.

'Ms...?'

'Collins. Penelope Collins.'

'Rafe Edwards.' The handshake was brief but surprisingly firm. This time she noticed his invitation and he watched her seat herself on one of the couches. Right on the edge as if she might need to leap up and flee at any moment. Legs angled but not crossed.

Nice legs. Was that subtle tug on the hem of her skirt because she'd noticed him noticing? Rafe glanced at his watch and then seated himself on the opposite couch. Or rather perched on his favourite spot, with a hip resting on the broad arm of the couch.

'So...a celebrity wedding?'

She nodded. 'You've heard of Clarissa Bingham?'

'Can't say I have.'

'Oh… She's a local Loxbury girl who got famous in a reality TV show. She's marrying a football star. Blake Summers.'

'I've heard of *him*.'

'It's a huge wedding and we were lucky enough to get the best venue available. Loxbury Hall?'

'Yep. Heard of that, too.'

Her surprise was evident in the way she blinked—that rapid sweep of thick, dark eyelashes. He could understand the surprise. Why should he know anything about a small town on the outskirts of the New Forest between here and Southampton? Or an eighteenth-century manor house that had been used as a function venue for the last decade? He wasn't about to tell her that this location did, in fact, give him a rather close connection to this upcoming event.

'It could be the last wedding ever held there because the property's just been sold and nobody knows whether the new owner will carry it on as a business venture.'

'Hmm.' Rafe nodded but his attention was

straying. This Penelope Collins might not be re-motely his type but any red-blooded male could appreciate that she was beautiful. Classically beautiful with that golden blonde hair and that astonishing porcelain skin. Or maybe not so classical given that her eyes were brown rather than blue. Nice combination, that—blonde hair and brown eyes—and her skin had a sun-kissed glow to it that suggested an excellent spray tan rather than risking damage from the real thing. She was probably no more than five feet three without those killer heels and her drink of choice was probably a gin and tonic. Or maybe a martini with an olive placed perfectly in the centre of the toothpick.

'Sorry...what was that?'

'It's the perfect place for a fireworks show. The terrace off the ballroom looks down at the lake. There'll be six hundred people there and major magazine coverage. I could make sure that your company gets excellent publicity.'

'We tend to get that from our larger events. Or

special-effects awards from the movie industry. There are plenty of smaller companies out there that specialise in things like birthday parties or weddings.'

'But I want this to be spectacular. The *best*...'

She did. He could see that in her eyes. He'd had that kind of determination once—the need to get to the top and be the very best, and it hadn't been easy, especially that first time.

'Is this your first wedding?'

Her composure slipped and faint spots of pink appeared on her cheeks. 'I run a very successful catering company so I've been involved in big events for many years. Moving to complete event design and execution *has* been a more recent development.'

'So this *is* your first wedding.'

She didn't like the implied putdown. Something like defiance darkened her eyes and the aura of tension around the rest of her body kicked up a notch.

'The event is running like clockwork so far.

Everything's in place for the ceremony and reception. The entertainment, decorations and catering are locked in. Clarissa is thrilled with her dress and the photographers are over the moon by the backdrops the venue offers. We even have the best local band playing live for the dancing. You must have heard of Diversion?'

Rafe's breath came out in an unexpected huff. Another connection? This was getting weird.

'It was all going perfectly until this morning, when Clarissa decided they had to have fireworks to finish the night. She had a complete meltdown when I told her that it was probably impossible to organise at such late notice.'

Rafe had dealt with some meltdowns from clients so he knew how difficult it could be, especially when your reputation might be hanging by a thread. Maybe Penelope was reliving some of the tension and that was what was giving her voice that almost imperceptible wobble. A hint of vulnerability that tugged on something deep in his gut with an equally almost imperceptible 'ping'.

'When it got to the stage that she was threatening to pull the plug on the whole wedding, I said I'd make some enquiries.'

'So you came straight to the top?' The corner of Rafe's mouth lifted. 'Have to say your style is impressive, Ms Collins.'

He'd done the same thing himself more than once.

'I know I'm asking a lot and it probably is impossible but at least I can say I tried and…and maybe you can point me in the direction of an alternative company that might be able to do at least a reasonable job.'

There was a moment's silence as Rafe wondered how to respond. Yes, he could send her hunting for another company but nobody reputable would take this on.

'Have you any idea what's involved with setting up a professional fireworks show?'

She shook her head. She caught her bottom lip

between her teeth, too, and the childlike gesture of trepidation was enough to make Rafe wonder just how much of her look was a front. And what was she trying to hide?

'Long-term planning is essential for lots of reasons. We have to have meetings with the client to discuss budgets and the style and timing of the show.'

'The budget won't be an issue.'

'Are you sure? We're talking over a thousand pounds a minute here.'

'I'm sure.' She sounded confident but he'd seen the movement of her throat as she'd swallowed hard.

'The show gets fired to music. That has to be chosen and then edited and correlated to the pyrotechnic effects. The soundtrack has to be cued and programmed into a computer.'

Once upon a time, Rafe had done all these jobs himself. Long, hard nights of getting everything perfect on an impossible schedule. The memories weren't all bad, though. That kind of hard work had got him where he was today.

'The fireworks have to be chosen and sourced. The site has to be mapped and the display layout planned for firing points. There are safety considerations and you have to allow for a fallout range that could be over a hundred metres. You have to get permits. And this all has to happen before you start setting up—fusing all the fireworks together in the correct sequence, putting electric matches in each fuse run, and then testing the whole package to make sure it's going to work.'

'I understand.' There was a stillness about her that suggested she was preparing to admit defeat. 'And you were right. I had no idea how much work was involved. I'm sorry…' She got to her feet. 'It was very kind of you to take the time to explain things.'

The door to the office opened as she finished speaking. Melissa poked her head around the edge.

'They're waiting for you in the boardroom, Mr Edwards.'

Rafe got to his feet, too. Automatically, he held out his hand and Penelope took it. It was a clasp rather than a shake and, for some bizarre reason, Rafe found himself holding her hand for a heartbeat longer than could be considered professional.

Long enough for that odd ping of sensation he'd felt before to return with surprising force. Enough force to be a twist that couldn't be dismissed. A memory of what it was like to be struggling and then come up against a brick wall? Or maybe articulating all the steps of the challenge of delivering a show had reminded him that he'd been able to do all that himself once. Every single job that he now employed experts in the field to do on his behalf.

He could do it again if he wanted. Good grief, he ran one of the biggest pyrotechnic companies in the world—he could do whatever he wanted.

And maybe…he wanted to do *this*.

He had everything he'd always dreamed of now but this wasn't the first time he'd felt that niggle that something was missing. Wasn't the best way to find something to retrace your footsteps? Going back to his roots as a young pyrotechnician would certainly be retracing footsteps that were long gone. Had he dropped something so long ago he'd forgotten what it actually was?

'There is one way I might be able to help,' he found himself saying.

'A personal recommendation to another company?' Hope made her eyes shine. They had a dark outline to their pupils, he noticed. Black on brown. A perfect ring to accentuate them. Striking.

'No. I was thinking more in terms of doing it myself.'

Her breath caught in an audible gasp. 'But… all those things you said…'

'They still stand. Whether or not it's doable would depend on cooperation from your clients with any restrictions, such as what fireworks we happen to have in stock. The site survey and decisions on style and music would have to be done immediately. Tomorrow.'

'I could arrange that.' That breathless excitement in her voice was sweet. 'What time would you be available?'

'It's Saturday. We don't have any major shows happening and I make my own timetable. What time would your clients be available?'

'We'll be on site all day. They have a dance lesson in the morning and we're doing a ceremony rehearsal in the afternoon. Just come anytime that suits. Would you like me to email you a map?'

'That won't be necessary. By coincidence, I'm familiar with the property, which is another point in favour of pulling this off. The site survey wouldn't be an issue.'

The massive image of exploding fireworks was impossible to miss as Penelope left the office but it was more than simply a glorious advertisement now. For a heartbeat, it felt like she was actually *there*—seeing them happen and hearing the bone-shaking impact of the detonations.

Excitement, that was what it was. Ralph Edwards might look like a cowboy but he was going to help her get the biggest break she could ever have. Clarissa's wedding was going to finish with the kind of bang that would have her at the top of any list of desirable wedding planners. On her way to fame and fortune and a lifelong career that couldn't be more perfect for her. She would be completely independent and then she'd be able to decide what else she might need in her life.

Who else, maybe…

Thanks to the traffic, the drive back to Loxbury was going to take well over two hours, which meant she would be up very late tonight, catching up with her schedule. She could use the time sensibly and think ahead about any potential troubleshooting that might be needed.

Or she could think about fireworks instead. The kind of spectacular shapes and colours that would be painted against the darkness of a rural sky but probably seen by every inhabitant of her nearby hometown and have images reproduced in more than one glossy magazine.

As the miles slid by—despite an odd initial resistance—Penelope also found herself thinking about the tousled cowboy she would have to be working with in the coming week to make this happen. He had to be the most unlikely colleague she could have imagined. Someone she would have instinctively avoided like the plague under normal circumstances, even. But if he could help her make this wedding the event that would launch her career, she was up for it.

Couldn't wait to see him again, in fact.

CHAPTER TWO

'No, no, Monsieur Blake. Do not bend over your lady like that, or you will lose your balance and you will both end up on the floor. Step to the side and bend your knee as you dip her. Keep your back *straight*.'

Blake Summers abruptly let go of his bride-to-be but Clarissa caught his arm. 'Don't you dare walk out on me again. How are we ever going to learn this dance if you keep walking away?'

He shook his arm free. 'I can't do it, babe. I told you that. I. Don't. Dance.'

'But this our *wedding* dance.' The tone advertised imminent tears. 'Everyone will be watching. Taking photos.'

'This whole thing is all about the photos, isn't it? I'm up to *here* with it.' Muscles in the young football star's arm bunched as he raised a fist well above head level. 'You know what? If I'd had any idea of how much crap this would all involve I would have thought twice about asking you to marry me.'

'Oh, my God…' Clarissa buried her face in her hands and started sobbing. Penelope let out a long sigh. She felt rather inclined to follow her example.

The dance teacher, Pierre, came towards her with a wonderfully French gesture that described exactly how frustrated he was also becoming.

'It's only a simple dance,' he muttered. 'We've been here for an hour and we have only covered the first twenty seconds of the song. Do you know how long Monsieur Legend's "All of Me" goes for?' He didn't wait for Penelope to respond. 'Five minutes and eight seconds—that's how long. *C'est de la torture.*'

Blake's expression morphed from anger to irritation and finally defeat. 'I'm sorry, babe. I didn't mean it. Really.' He put his arms around Clarissa.

'I just meant we could have eloped or something and got away from all the fuss.'

'You did mean it.' Clarissa struggled enough to escape his embrace. 'You don't want to marry me.' She turned her back on him and hugged herself tightly.

'I do. I love you, babe. All of me, you know, loves all of you.'

Clarissa only sobbed louder. This was Penelope's cue to enter stage left. She walked briskly across the polished wood of the floor and put an arm around her client's shoulders.

'It's okay, hon. We just need to take a break.' She gave a squeeze. 'It's such an emotional time in the final run-up to such a big day. Things can seem a bit overwhelming, can't they?'

Clarissa nodded, sniffing loudly.

'And we've got a whole week to sort this dance out. Just a few moves that you can repeat for the whole song, isn't that right, Pierre?'

Pierre shrugged. 'As you say. Only a few moves.'

Penelope turned her most encouraging smile

on the groom-to-be. 'You're up for that, aren't you, Blake? You do know how incredibly sexy it is for a man to be able to dance, even a little bit, don't you?'

'Dancing's for pansies,' Blake muttered.

Penelope's smile dimmed. She could feel a vibe coming from Pierre's direction that suggested she might be about to lose her on-call dance teacher.

'How 'bout this?' she suggested brightly. 'We'll put the music on and Pierre will dance with Clarissa to show you what you'll look like on the night. So you can see how romantic it will be. How gorgeous you'll both look.'

Blake scowled but Clarissa was wiping tears from her face with perfectly French-manicured fingertips. The sideways glance at the undeniably good-looking dance teacher was flirtatious enough for Penelope to be thankful that Blake didn't seem to notice.

'Fine.' He walked towards the tall windows that doubled as doors to the flagged terrace. Penelope joined him as Pierre set the music up and talked to Clarissa.

'Gorgeous view, isn't it?'

'I guess. The lake's okay. I like those dragons that spout water.'

'The whole garden's wonderful. You should have a look around while the weather's this nice. There's even a maze.'

The notes of the romantic song filled the space as Pierre swept Clarissa into his arms and began leading her expertly through the moves. Blake crossed his arms and scowled.

'It's easy for her. She's been doing salsa classes for years. But she expects me to look like *him*? Not going to happen. Not in this lifetime.'

Penelope shook her head and smiled gently. 'I think all she wants is to be moving to the song she's chosen in the arms of the man she loves.'

A sound of something like resignation came from Blake but Penelope could feel the tension lift. Until his head turned and he stiffened again.

'Who's that?' he demanded. 'I told you I didn't

want anyone watching this lesson. I feel like enough of an idiot as it is. If that's a photographer, hoping to get a shot of me practising, he can just get the hell out of here.'

Penelope turned her head. The ballroom of Loxbury Hall ran the length of the house between the two main wings. There were probably six huge bedrooms above it upstairs. Quite some distance to recognise a shadowy figure standing in the doorway that led to the reception hall but she knew who it was instantly. From the man's height, perhaps. Or the casual slouch to his stance. That shaft of sensation deep in her belly had to be relief. He'd kept his word.

She could trust him?

'It's Ralph Edwards!' she exclaimed softly. 'I told you he was coming some time today. To discuss your fireworks?'

'Oh…yeah…' Blake's scowl vanished. 'Fireworks are cool.' He brightened. 'Does that mean I don't have to do any more dancing today?'

'Let's see what Pierre's schedule is. We'd have

time for another session later. After the meeting with the florist maybe. Before the rehearsal.'

It was another couple of minutes before the song ended. Clarissa was following Pierre's lead beautifully and Penelope tried to focus, letting her imagination put her client into her wedding dress. To think how it was going to look with the soft lighting of hundreds of candles. The song was a great choice. If Blake could end up learning the moves well enough to look a fraction as good as Pierre, it was going to be a stunning first dance.

Details flashed into her mind, like the best places to put the huge floral arrangements and groups of candles to frame the dance floor. Where the photographers and cameramen could be placed to be inconspicuous but still get great coverage. Whether it was going to work to have the wrist loop to hold the train of Clarissa's dress out of the way. She scribbled a note on the paper clipped to the board she carried with her everywhere on days like this so that none of these details would end up being forgotten.

The dress. Candles. Flowers. There was so much to think about and yet the thing she was most aware of right now was the figure standing at the ballroom doorway, politely waiting for the music to finish before interrupting. Why did his presence make her feel so nervous? Her heart had picked up speed the moment she'd seen him and it hadn't slowed any since. That initial twinge of relief had shattered into butterflies in her stomach now, and they were twisting and dancing rather like Clarissa was.

Not that the feeling was altogether unpleasant. It reminded her of the excitement that strong physical attraction to someone could produce.

Was she physically attracted to Ralph Edwards?

Of course not. The very idea was so ridiculous she knew that wasn't the cause. No. This nervousness was because the fireworks show wasn't a done deal yet and there could be another tantrum from Clarissa to handle if the meeting didn't go well.

It had to go well. Penelope held the clipboard against her chest and clutched it a little more tightly as the music faded.

Rafe was quite content to have a moment or two to observe.

To bask in the glow of satisfaction he'd had from the moment he'd driven through the ornate gates of this historic property.

A property he now owned, for heaven's sake.

Who would have thought that he'd end up with a life like this? Not him, that's for sure. Not back in the day when he'd been one of a busload of disadvantaged small children who'd been brought to Loxbury Hall for a charity Christmas party. He'd seen the kind of kingdom that rich people could have. People with enough money to make their own rules. To have families that stayed together and lived happily ever after.

Yes. This was a dream come true and he was loving every minute of it.

He was loving standing here, too.

This room was stunning. A few weeks ago he'd had to use his imagination to think of what it might be like with music playing and people dancing on the polished floor. Reality was even better. He was too far away to get more than a general impression of the girl who was dancing but he could see enough. A wild cascade of platinum blonde waves. A tight, low-cut top that revealed a cleavage to die for. Enhanced by silicone, of course, but what did that matter? She was a true WAG and Blake Summers was a lucky young man.

What a contrast to Ms Collins—standing there clutching a clipboard and looking as tense as a guitar string about to snap. You'd never get her onto a dance floor as a partner, that's for sure. His buoyant mood slipped a little—kind of reminding him of schooldays when the bell sounded and you had to leave the playground and head back to the classroom.

Never mind. As she'd pointed out herself, this could well be the last time the reception rooms of Loxbury Hall would be used as a public venue and there was a kind of irony in the idea that he could be putting on a fireworks show to mark the end of that era for the house and the start of his own occupation.

Remarkably fitting, really.

Rafe walked towards her as the music faded. Was her look supposed to be more casual, given that it was a weekend? If so, it hadn't worked. Okay, it was a shirt and trousers instead of a skirt but they were tailored and sleek and she still had that complicated rope effect going on in her hair. Did she sleep like that and still not have a hair out of place in the morning?

Maybe she didn't sleep at all. Just plugged herself in to a power point for a while.

Good thing that he was close enough to extend a hand to the young man standing beside Penelope. That way, nobody could guess that his grin was due to private amusement.

'I'm Rafe Edwards,' he said. 'Saw that winning goal you scored on your last match. Good effort.'

'Thanks, man. This is Clarissa. Clarrie, this is Ralph Edwards—the fireworks guy.'

'Rafe, please. I might have Ralph on my birth certificate but it doesn't mean I like it.' His smile widened as Clarissa batted ridiculously enhanced eyelashes at him and then he turned his head.

'Gidday, Penny. How are you?'

'Penelope,' she said tightly. 'I actually like the name on *my* birth certificate.'

Whoa…could she get any more uptight? Rafe turned back to the delicious Clarissa and turned on the charm.

'How 'bout we find somewhere we can get comfortable and have a chat about what I might be able to do for you?'

Clarissa giggled. 'Ooh…yes, *please*…'

'Why don't we go out onto the terrace?' Penelope's tone made the suggestion sound like a reprimand. 'I just need to have a word with Pierre and then I'll join you. I'll organise some refreshment, too. What would you like?'

'Mineral water for me,' Clarissa said. 'Sparkling.'

'A cold beer,' Blake said. 'It's turning into a scorcher of a day.'

'I'm not sure we've got beer in the kitchen at the moment.'

Blake groaned.

'My apologies,' Penelope said. 'I'll make sure it's available next time.' She scribbled something on her clipboard.

'Coffee for me, thanks,' Rafe said. 'Strong and black.'

The look flashed in his direction was grateful. 'That we *can* do. Would you like a coffee, too, Blake?'

'Have to do, I s'pose. At least we're gonna get to talk about something cool. Do we get to choose the kind of fireworks we want?'

'Sure. We need to talk about the music first,

though.' Rafe led the way through the French doors to the terrace. 'I'm guessing you want something romantic?'

Music wasn't being discussed when Penelope took the tray of drinks out to the group. Rafe had a laptop open and Blake and Clarissa were avidly watching what was on the screen.

'Ooh…that one. We've got to have that. What's it called?'

'It's a peony. And this one's a chrysanthemum. And this is a golden, hanging willow. It's a forty-five-shot cake so it goes for a while.'

'Nice. I like them loud.' Blake was rubbing his hands together. 'Man, this is going to be epic.'

'With it being your wedding, I was thinking you might want something a bit more romantic.' Rafe tapped his keyboard. 'Look at this for an opening, maybe.'

'OMG.' Clarissa pressed a hand to her open mouth. 'You can do love hearts? For *real*?'

'Sure can. And look at this. Horsetails look a lot like bridal veils, don't you think?'

Clarissa hadn't looked this happy since the first fitting of her wedding dress. Before she'd started to find tiny imperfections that had to be dealt with.

'I want it to be romantic,' she breathed. 'And I've got the perfect song. Whitney Houston's "I Will Always Love You".'

Blake rolled his eyes and shook his head. Rafe lifted an eyebrow. 'Nice, but the tempo could be a bit on the slow side. Maybe a better song to dance to than accompany fireworks?'

'It's soppy,' Blake growled. 'We need something loud. Fun. Wasn't the whole idea to end the night with a bang?'

Clarissa giggled. 'Oh…we will, babes, don't you worry about that.'

Blake grinned. 'You're singing my song already.'

Rafe's appreciative grin faded the moment

he caught Penelope's gaze. He took a sip of his coffee.

'What about Meat Loaf?' Blake suggested. '"I'd Do Anything For Love"?'

'Not bad. Good beats to time to effects.'

'No.' Clarissa shook her head firmly.

Penelope was searching wildly for inspiration. 'Bon Jovi? "Livin' On A Prayer"? Or the Troggs? "Wild Thing"?'

'Getting better.' Rafe nodded. The look he gave her this time held a note of surprise. Did he think she wasn't into music or something? 'Let's keep it going. Bon Jovi's a favourite of mine. What about "Always"?'

The words of the song drifted into Penelope's head. Along with an image of it being passionately sung. And even though it was Rafe she was looking at, it was no excuse to let her mind drift to imagining him with wild, rock-god hair. Wearing a tight, black singlet and frayed jeans. Saying he would cry for the woman he loved. Or die for her...

Phew…it was certainly getting hot. She fanned herself with her clipboard and tried to refocus. To push any image of men in frayed jeans and singlets out of her head. So not her type.

She liked designer suits and neat haircuts. The kind of up-and-coming young attorney look, like her last boyfriend who'd not only graduated from law school with honours but was active in a major political party. Disappointing that it had turned out they'd had nothing in common—especially for her grandparents—but she didn't have time for a relationship in her life right now anyway.

She didn't have time to pander to this group's inability to reach an agreement either, but she couldn't think of any way to speed things up and half an hour later they were still no closer to making a definitive choice.

Further away, perhaps, given that both Clarissa and Blake were getting annoyed enough to veto any suggestion the other made and getting steadily snarkier about it. Any moment now it would erupt into a full-blown row and the hint of annoyance in Rafe's body language would turn into disgust and he'd walk away from a job he didn't actually need.

Penelope was increasingly aware that time was running out. They had a meeting with the florist coming up, Pierre was going to return for another dance lesson and there was a rehearsal with the celebrant in the garden at four p.m.

'Did you have anything else you needed to do while you're here?' she asked Rafe.

'A bit of a survey.' He nodded. 'I need to get a feel for the layout and check where I'd position things. I'm thinking a barge on the other side of the lake but I'll be able to get a good view if I go upstairs and—' He stopped abruptly. 'Is that a problem?'

'We're not allowed upstairs,' Clarissa confided. 'Apparently it's one of the biggest rules about using this venue.'

'Is that right?'

It was no surprise that Rafe wasn't impressed by a set of rules and his tone suggested he wouldn't hesitate in breaking them. She could imagine how well it would go down if she forbade the action and she certainly didn't want to get him offside any more than he was already, thanks to the sparring young couple.

If he had to go upstairs in order to be able to do his job, maybe she'd just have to turn a blind eye and hope for the best. At least she could plead ignorance of it actually happening if word got out and she could probably apologise well enough to smooth things over if the owners were upset.

'How long will your survey take?' The words came out more crisply than she'd intended.

'Thirty-nine minutes.' He grinned. 'No, make that forty-one.'

He wasn't the only person getting annoyed here. 'In that case, let's meet back here in forty-five minutes,' Penelope said. 'Blake—take Clarissa to the Loxbury pub and you can get your cold beer and a quick lunch and see if you can agree on a song. This fireworks show isn't going to happen unless we lock that in today. Isn't that right, Ralph?'

His look was deadpan.

'Sorry. Rafe.'

'That's right, Penelope. We're on a deadline that's tight enough to be almost impossible as it is.' He smiled at Clarissa. 'You want your red hearts exploding all over the sky to start the show. What if I told you we could put both your names inside a love heart to finish?'

Clarissa looked like she'd just fallen in love with this new acquaintance. She tugged on Blake's arm with some urgency. 'Come on, babes. We've *got* to find a song.'

'I'll have a think, too,' Penelope called after them. 'I've got my iPod and I need a bit of a walk.'

There was a third-floor level on each of the wings of the house, set back enough to provide an up-stairs terraced area. Rafe fancied one of these rooms as his bedroom and that was where he headed. He already knew that he'd have the best view of the lake and garden from that terrace. It took a few minutes to get there. Was he crazy, thinking he could actually live in a place this big?

By himself?

He had plenty of friends, he reminded himself as he stepped over the braided rope on the stairs marking the boundary of public access. The guys in the band would want to make this place party central. And it wasn't as if he'd be here that much. He had his apartments in New York and London and he was looking at getting one in China, given that he spent a lot of time there sourcing fireworks. He'd need staff, too. No way could he manage a house this size. And he'd probably need an entire team of full-time gardeners, he decided as he stepped out onto the bedroom terrace. Just clipping the hedges of that maze would probably keep someone busy for weeks.

In fact, there was someone in there right now. Rafe walked closer to the stone pillars edging the terrace and narrowed his eyes. The figure seemed to know its way through the maze, moving swiftly until it reached the grass circle that marked the centre.

Penelope. Of course it was. Hadn't she said she needed a walk? She stopped for a moment with her head down, fiddling with something in her hand. Her iPod? And then she pressed her fingertips against her ears as though she was listening carefully to whatever music she had chosen.

Rafe should have been scanning the grounds on the far side of the lake and thinking about positioning things like the scissor lift he'd need to hold the frame for the lancework of doing the names in fireworks to end the show. Instead, he found himself watching Penelope.

She was kicking her shoes off, which was probably sensible given that heels would sink into that grass. But then she did something that made Rafe's jaw drop. Blew whatever it was he'd been thinking of her right out of the water.

She started dancing.

Not just the kind of unconscious jiggle along with the beat either. She was dancing like she thought no one could see her which was probably exactly what she did think, tucked into the centre of that maze with its tall, thick hedges.

Rafe leaned into the corner of the terrace, any thoughts of planning a show escaping irretrievably. His eyes narrowed as he focused on the slim figure moving on her secret stage.

An amused snort escaped him. No wonder she needed to hide herself away. She was rubbish at dancing. Her movements were uncoordinated enough to probably make her a laughing stock on a dance floor.

But then his amusement faded. She was doing something she believed was private and she was doing it with her heart and soul. Maybe she didn't really know how to dance but she was doing more than just hearing that music—she was a part of it with every cell of her body.

Rafe knew that feeling. That ability to lose yourself in sound so completely the rest of the world disappeared. Music could be an anaesthetic that made even the worst kind of pain bearable.

Impossible not to remember wearing headphones and turning the sound level up so loud that nothing else existed. So you couldn't hear the latest row erupting in the new foster home that meant you'd be packed up before long and handed around again like some unwanted parcel.

Impossible not to still feel grateful for that first set of drums he'd been gifted so many years ago. Or the thrill of picking up a saxophone for the first time and starting the journey that meant he could do more than simply listen. That meant he could become a part of that music.

It was another world. One that had saved him from what this one had seemed doomed to become.

And he was getting the same feeling from watching Penelope being uninhibited enough to try and dance.

What was that about?

He'd sensed that what you could see with Penelope Collins wasn't necessarily real, hadn't he? When she'd admitted she knew nothing about setting up a fireworks show. Watching her now made him more sure that she was putting up a front to hide who she really was.

Who was the person that was hiding?

Or maybe the real question here was why did he want to know?

He didn't.

With a jerk, Rafe straightened and forced his gaze sideways towards the lake and the far shore. Was there enough clearance from the trees to put a scissor lift or two on the ground or would the safety margins require a barge on the water? He'd bring one of the lads out here first thing tomorrow and they could use a range finder to get accurate measurements but he could trust his eye for now. And he just happened to have an aerial photograph of the property on his laptop, too. Pulling a notepad and the stub of a pencil from the back pocket of his jeans, he started sketching.

By the time he'd finished what he'd wanted to

do he was five minutes late for the time they'd agreed to meet back on the terrace. Not that it made him hurry down the stairs or anything but he wouldn't have planned to stop before he turned into the ballroom and headed for the terrace. The thought only occurred to him when he saw the iPod lying on the hall table, on top of that clipboard Penelope carried everywhere with her.

If he took a look at what she'd played recently, could he pick what it was that she'd been dancing to? Get some kind of clue to solve the puzzle of who this woman actually was?

Clarissa and Blake were late getting back from lunch and, judging by the looks on their faces, they hadn't managed to agree on the music to accompany their fireworks show.

Which meant that Rafe would most likely pull the plug on doing it at all.

He came through the French doors from the ballroom at the same time as the young couple were climbing the stairs from the garden.

'Did you decide?' Rafe asked.

'We tried,' Clarissa groaned. 'We really did...' Her face brightened. 'But then we thought you're the expert. We'll let you decide.'

Penelope bit back the suggestion she'd been about to make. Throwing ideas around again would only take them back to square one and this was a potentially quick and easy fix.

But Rafe lifted an eyebrow. 'You sure about that? Because I reckon I've found the perfect song.'

'What is it?'

'Doesn't matter,' Blake growled. 'You promised you wouldn't argue this time.'

'Have a listen,' Rafe said, putting his laptop on the table and flipping it open. He tapped rapidly on the keyboard. 'I think you might like it.'

It only took the first two notes for Penelope to recognise the song and it sent a chill down her spine. The very song she'd been about to suggest herself. How spooky was *that*?

'Ohhh…' Clarissa's eyes were huge. 'I *love* this song.'

'Who is that?' Blake was frowning. 'Celine Dion?'

Rafe shook his head. 'This is the original version. Jennifer Rush. She cowrote "The Power of Love" in 1984.'

It was the version that Penelope preferred. The one she had on her iPod. The one she'd been dancing to in her private space in the centre of the maze only half an hour or so ago, when she'd taken that much-needed break.

'It's got some great firing points. Like that…' Rafe's hands prescribed an arc as the crescendo started. 'And we can use the extended version to give us a good length of time. Fade it away to leave your names in the heart hanging over the lake.'

He wasn't looking at Penelope. He didn't even send a triumphant glance in her direction as Clarissa and Blake enthusiastically agreed to the song choice.

Which was probably just as well. Penelope had no idea what her expression might look like but it had to include an element of shock. Surely it had to be more than coincidence and she didn't believe in telepathy but it was impossible not to feel some sort of weird connection happening here. How awful would it be if she looked like Clarissa had when he'd told her he could finish the show by putting their names in a love heart? As though she'd just fallen head over heels in love with the man?

Not that it really mattered. The *pièce de résistance* of the wedding that was going to launch her new career was starting to come together and the choice of song was perfect.

With a lot of hard work and a little bit more luck, this whole wedding was going to be perfect.

CHAPTER THREE

SO FAR, SO GOOD.

They couldn't have wished for a better day weather-wise for what the local media was already billing the wedding of the year. The blue stretch of summer sky was broken only by innocent cotton-wool puffs of cloud and it was warm enough for the skimpy dresses most of the women seemed to be wearing. More importantly, the breeze was gentle enough not to ruin any elaborate hairdos or play havoc with a bridal veil.

The vintage champagne every guest had been offered on arrival was going down a treat and people were now beginning to drift towards the rows of chairs draped with white satin and tied with silver bows. Penelope saw someone open the small gauze bag she'd found on her seat and smile as she showed her partner the confetti that was made up of tiny, glittery silver stars.

How much bigger were those smiles going to be when they were watching the kind of stars that would explode across the sky as the finale to this event? Rafe had arrived as early as Penelope had, driving onto the estate in the chill mist of a breaking dawn. She'd seen him and the technicians he'd brought with him, in their fluorescent vests, working in the field on the far side of the lake at various times over the hectic hours since then. Just orange dots of humanity, really, at this distance, but she was sure it was Rafe who was directing the forklift manoeuvring the pallets from the back of a truck at one point and, much later, the towing of a flat barge to float on the lake.

Because that was the kind of job a boss would do, she told herself. It had nothing to do with that odd tingle of something she had no intention of trying to identify. A tingle that appeared along with that persistent image of the man in frayed jeans and a black singlet she had conjured up. An image that had insisted on haunting her dreams over the last week, leaving her to wake with the odd sensation that something was simply not *fair*…

Heading back inside the house, she popped into the kitchen to check that her team was on top of the catering. Judging by the numerous silver platters of hors d'oeuvres lined up ready for the lull while photographs would be taken after the ceremony, they were right on schedule.

'Any worries, Jack?'

'Apart from an eight-course sit-down dinner for two hundred and supper for six hundred? Nah… it's all good.' The older man's smile was reassuring. 'I've got this side of the gig covered. Go and play with your bride.'

'I do need to do that. But I'll be back later. Keep an apron for me.'

'Are you kidding? That dress is far too fancy to get hidden by any apron.'

'It's not too much, is it?' Penelope glanced down at the dark silver sheath dress she had chosen. A lot of effort had gone into what she hoped would be her signature outfit as she occupied an unusual space in a wedding party that was more than simply hired help but less than invited guest. The dress was demure with its long sleeves and scooped neckline that only showed a hint of cleavage. The skirt was ballet length and fell in soft swirls from thigh level but it did fit like a glove everywhere else and it had a soft sparkle that would probably intensify under artificial or candle light.

Jack grinned. 'You look like the director of the nation's most successful event managing company. Make sure they get some photos of you for one of those flash magazines. Now—stop distracting me. Get out of my kitchen and go and keep our first event ticking. Isn't Princess Clarissa about due for another meltdown?'

'Oh, God, I hope not.' With a worried frown, Penelope headed for a ground-floor room in the west wing that had been set aside for the bride and bridesmaids to get dressed in. A room in the east wing was where the groom and his entourage were waiting. That would be the next stop, to make sure they were in position on time. Penelope checked her watch. Only twenty minutes away. The countdown was on.

She took a deep breath. At least she didn't have to worry about the catering side of things. Jack— her head chef—had worked with her ever since she'd advertised for someone to come on board with a fledgling catering company nearly ten years ago. His own restaurant might have failed despite his talent with food but together they'd built a company to be proud of and it had been his idea for her to take the risky move of taking on event management.

Dreaming about something and even making endless lists of the things that she'd have to keep on top of hadn't really prepared her for the reality of it, though. The catering was only one aspect. Had the celebrant arrived yet? Were the photographers behaving themselves? How were the band going in setting themselves up? She'd seen the truck parked around the back an hour or more ago and people unloading a drum kit and amplifiers but what if they couldn't find enough power points? There was a lighting expert who was coming to supervise the safe positioning and lighting of all those candles and would then be in charge for any spotlighting of key people. He hadn't arrived as far as she knew but they weren't due to meet until after the actual ceremony.

At some point, she would have to find Rafe, too, and make sure that he was happy with his set-up. The fireworks were scheduled to go off at one a.m. to mark the end of the party and there was plenty of security personnel discreetly in place to make sure nobody went into forbidden areas and that everybody left Loxbury Hall when they were supposed to.

It was possible that this was the moment when the tension was at its highest. The moment before the carefully timed show that was going to be the wedding of the year kicked off. With her heart in her mouth, Penelope opened the door of the bride's dressing room. Clarissa—in a froth of white—was standing serenely in the centre of the room with a champagne flute in her hand. She was surrounded by her six bridesmaids who were in same shade of orange as one of the colours of Blake's football club. One of the girls sent another champagne cork hurtling towards the ceiling with a loud pop and the shriek of happy giggles was deafening. The flash of the camera from the official photographer showed he was capturing every joyous moment.

The hairdresser and make-up artists and their teams were packing up an enormous amount of gear. Hair straighteners, heated rollers and cans of spray went into one set of suitcases. Pots of foundation, dozens of brushes and cards of false eyelashes were heading for another. Penelope smiled at the women.

'I think you deserve to join the celebration. They all look fabulous.' She stepped closer and lowered her voice, although it was hardly necessary as the chatter and laughter as the glasses were being refilled were enough to make any conversation private. 'Any problems?'

Cheryl's smile said it all. 'Bit of a mission to get every one of Clarissa's curls sitting just right but we got there in the end. Thank goodness for industrial-strength hairspray.'

The spirals of platinum blonde hair hung to the bride's waist at the back, easily visible through the sheer mist of an exquisitely embroidered veil. Tresses at the front had been twisted and clipped into a soft frame that supported the tiara holding the veil, as well as offering an anchor for a dozen or more small silver stars. A star made of diamonds sparkled on the perfect spray tan of Clarissa's décolletage—a gift from Blake that had inspired one of the themes for the wedding. Beneath that, the heavily beaded corset bodice of the dress made the most of what had to be close to the top of the bride's assets.

'What d'ya think, Penelope?'

'I think you couldn't look more perfect, Clarrie. It's just as well Blake's got all those groomsmen to hold him up when he sees you walking down the aisle.' She took another quick glance at her watch. 'Five minutes and we'll need you all in position in the reception hall. I'm just going to make sure the boys are out of the building and that those photographs as you come out will be the first glimpse of your dress that the world gets.'

It was Penelope who waited with Clarissa in the main entrance, signalling each pair of bridesmaids when it was their turn to walk out of the huge doorway, down the sweep of wide steps and start the journey along the carpet that led to the raised gazebo where the celebrant was waiting, flanked by the males of the wedding party. Clarissa's song choice of Whitney Houston that had been rejected for the fireworks show was perfect for this entrance but it needed careful timing to make sure the bride arrived beside her groom before the song finished.

Penelope waited until all the heads turned to watch Clarissa take her final position, facing Blake and holding both his hands. Nobody saw her as she quietly made her way to the shade of an ancient oak tree, well away from the audience but close enough to hear the ceremony, thanks to the lapel microphone the celebrant was wearing.

A brief respite from the tension of the day was more than welcome. A private moment to collect her thoughts and remember to breathe.

Except it didn't stay private for long. A figure materialised beside her in the shade. A dark figure. And Penelope forgot to breathe for rather too long.

Had Rafe dressed up for the occasion? He was wearing black jeans today, and a black T-shirt that had a faded image of what was probably an album cover from a forgotten era. The cowboy boots were the same, though, and they were in harmony with a battered, wide-brimmed leather hat that any cowboy would have treasured.

He was dressed for his work and clearly comfortable with being on the hired-help side of the boundary Penelope was balancing on but right now her position in this gathering was unimportant. This short period of time was a limbo where nothing mattered other than the vows the wedding couple were exchanging. This tiny patch of the famous Loxbury Hall gardens was a kind of limbo as well. An island that only she and Rafe were inhabiting.

He was as dark as she was pale. As scruffy as she was groomed. As relaxed as she was tense. Black and white. Total opposites.

It should be making her feel very uncomfortable but it wasn't.

There was a curl of something pleasant stealing through Penelope's body. Try as she might to deny it, the surprise of his company was sprinkled with a condiment that could—quite disturbingly—be delight.

He'd had something on the tip of his tongue to justify the choice of joining Ms Collins in the shade of this tree. Had it been something about it being the best vantage point to observe the ceremony and that he had the time because everything else that could be a distraction in the background had to be put on hold for the duration? Not that his team had much else to do. Everything was in place and all that was needed between now and about midnight was a rehearsal to check that all the electronic components were in functioning order.

Or maybe it had been something about how well the event was going so far. That it was everything the perfect wedding should be.

No wonder the ability to produce words seemed to have failed him for the moment. This was everything the perfect wedding *shouldn't* be. The epitome of the circus that represented conforming to one of society's expected rules of declaring commitment and faithfulness. A rule that was rarely kept, so why bother with the circus in the first place?

Or perhaps the loss of a conversational opening had something to do with being this close to Penelope?

He'd spotted her discreet position from the edge of the lake where he'd initially positioned himself to be out of sight of the guests. That silvery dress she was wearing shone like a new moon in the dense shade of this ancient tree and…and it was possibly the most stunning dress he'd ever seen. Weird, considering there was no more cleavage to be seen than a tiny, teasing line just where that sun-kissed skin began to swell.

Rafe dragged his gaze away, hopefully before she was aware of his appreciation because the glance had been so swift. Her hair looked different today, too. Softer. She still had those braids shaping the sides of her head but the length of it was loose at the back, falling in a thick ringlet instead of another braid. It was longer than he remembered, almost touching the small of her back in that second, silver skin. What would happen, he found himself wondering, if he buried his fingers in that perfect silky spiral and pulled it apart? Would her whole back get covered with golden waves?

What was more likely to happen was that he would infuriate this would-be queen of event management by messing up her hair. She might not be holding a clipboard right now but the tension was still palpable. She was in control. On top of every moment and ready to troubleshoot any problem with the efficiency of a nuclear blast.

Clarissa's breathlessly excited whisper was being amplified by strategically placed microphones. 'I, Clarissa Grace Bingham, take thee, Blake Robert Summers, to be my lawfully wedded husband. To have and to hold...'

Finally, he found something to say.

'Sounds like she's the happiest girl on earth right now.'

'Of course she is. This is her wedding day. Every girl's dream.'

'Really?' Rafe couldn't help the note of scepticism. 'Does anyone really believe that those vows mean anything these days?'

Uh-oh… Maybe he should have ruffled the spiral of hair down her back instead of dropping some kind of verbal bomb. The look he received made him feel like he'd just told a kid that Santa Claus didn't really exist.

'I believe it,' Penelope said.

She did. He could see it in her eyes. A fierce belief that it meant something. Something important. He couldn't look away. He even found himself leaning a little closer as a soft word of query escaped his lips.

'Why?'

Oh, help… His eyes weren't really as black as sin, were they? The mottled light sifting down through the leaves of the tree was enough to reveal that they were a dark brown, with flecks of gold that made them more like a very deep hazel. And the way he was looking at her…

The eye contact had gone on far too long to be polite but Penelope couldn't break the gaze. It felt physical—almost as though he was holding her in his arms. No…it went deeper than that. He was holding something that wasn't physical. Touching something that was deep inside. The part of her that couldn't be seen.

But Rafe was seeing it and it made her feel… vulnerable?

Nobody had ever looked at her like this. As if they could see that dark, secret part of her. As if the world wouldn't end if the door got opened and light flooded in.

And he wanted to know why she believed in something he clearly had no time for. Marriage. Could he see that she *had* to believe in it? Because there was something about it that held the key to putting things right?

The exchange of vows had been completed on the stage of the gazebo and the applause and raucous whistling told her that the first kiss was happening. The flash of cameras going off was there, like stars in the periphery of her vision, but Penelope still couldn't look away from Rafe's gaze.

'It's about the promise,' she found herself saying softly. 'It's not about the dress or the flowers or…or even the fireworks.'

He raised an eyebrow.

'I don't mean they're not important. That's what weddings are all about. Celebrating the promise.' Penelope drew in a breath. She'd said enough and she should be using the time to make sure the photographers had everything they needed for the next part of the programme. And that Jack was ready to keep the guests entertained with food and wine for as long as it took. 'I can't wait to see the show,' she added with a placating smile. 'I know it'll be fabulous.'

'Oh, it will.' Rafe nodded. 'I'll make sure you get the best spot to watch it, shall I?'

'Won't you be busy? Pushing buttons or something?'

'There's pretty much only one button to push. On my laptop. The rest is automatic.'

'No problems setting up? It is all done?'

'Yes, ma'am.' He tipped his hat. 'We're about

to double-check everything and that'll be it until show time.'

'That's great. Thank you so much.' Penelope could see guests starting to move. Reaching for those bags of confetti stars and preparing to shower the bride and groom as they went down the aisle together. She stepped away to move closer but Rafe's voice stopped her.

'That promise,' he said quietly. 'The one you believe in. What is it, exactly?'

Startled, she turned her head. 'Security,' she responded. 'Family. It's the promise of a safe place, I guess. Somewhere you know you'll always be loved.'

There was something soft in his eyes now. Something sad?

'You're one of the lucky ones, then.'

'Because I believe in marriage?'

'Because you know what it's like to have a family. Parents. You know what it's like to live in that safe place.'

And he didn't? Something huge squeezed inside her chest and made her breath come out in a huff. She understood that yearning. Her life might look perfect from the outside but she wanted him to know that she understood. That they had a connection here that very few people could have. They might be complete opposites but in that moment it felt like they were the opposite sides of the same coin.

'I've never had parents. My mother abandoned me as a baby and then died. I have no idea who my father is.' Good grief…why on earth was she telling him this much? She backed off. 'You're right, though. I *was* lucky. My grandparents brought me up. I had everything I could possibly want.'

She saw the change in his eyes. He was backing off, too. Had he thought she understood but now saw her as one of the privileged? One who couldn't possibly have any idea of what it was like not to have that safe place?

Penelope didn't want to lose that tiny thread of connection. She was the one who needed that understanding, wasn't she? Because nobody had ever understood.

'Almost everything,' she added, her voice no more than a sigh. She swallowed past the tightness in her throat. 'Maybe if my parents had believed in marriage they could have looked after each other and things would have been different.' She bit her lip as the admission slipped out. 'Better...'

'You don't know that.' That softness in his gaze had changed. There was a flash of anger there. A world of pain. 'Things could have been worse.' Rafe tugged on the rim of his hat, blocking off his gaze. 'Catch you later,' he muttered as he turned away. 'When it's show time.'

The next hours were a blur. Penelope felt like she needed to be in six places at once to make sure everything was flowing smoothly but the adrenaline of it all kept her going without pause. A reporter from the magazine that had the exclusive, first coverage of the event even asked for a quick interview and photographs.

'You do realise you're going to be inundated with work after this, don't you? Every celebrity who's planning a wedding in the foreseeable future is going to want something this good.'

There was fear to be found hiding in the excitement of how well it was all going.

'We're a boutique company. I'm not ever going to take on more clients than I can personally take care of.'

'You've organised this all yourself?'

'I have a partner who's in charge of the catering today. Come and meet Jack. With dinner over, he should have a minute or two to spare. You could get a great picture of him in his chef's whites in the kitchen. He deserves the publicity as much as I do.'

'Let's get one of you two together.' The journalist made a note on her pad. 'Are you, like, a couple?'

Penelope shook her head as she smiled. 'No.

Jack has a family. I'm happily single. Career-woman, through and through, that's me.'

That was certainly the image she wanted to portray, anyway. There was no reason for anybody to ever feel sorry for Penelope Collins.

Not any more.

By midnight, the band had been playing for two hours and the party in the ballroom was still in full swing. The drums pulsed in Penelope's blood and the music was so good it was an effort not to let her body respond. It was just as well she was kept too occupied to do more than make a mental note to download some of Diversion's tracks so she could listen again in private.

People were getting drunk now. Emergency cleaning was needed more than once in the restrooms and an ambulance was discreetly summoned to the service entrance to remove one unconscious young woman. Another one was found sobbing in the garden and it fell to Penelope to sit and listen to the tale of romantic woe and calm the guest enough to rejoin the revelry.

Then she escaped to the kitchens for a while and insisted on an apron so she could spend a few minutes helping to prepare the supper that would be served on the terrace, timed to finish as the fireworks started.

And then it would all be over, bar the massive job of clearing up, most of which would happen tomorrow. All the tension and exhaustion of the last weeks and days and hours would be over. What was that going to feel like? Would she crawl home and crash or would she still be buzzing this time tomorrow?

Her head was spinning a little now, which suggested that it might be a good thing if she crashed. Maybe that glass of champagne with Jack a few minutes ago to toast their success had been a bad thing. At least it was quieter in the vast spaces of Loxbury Hall. The dance music was finished and people were crowded onto the terrace, enjoying a last glass or two of champagne, along with the delicious canapés on offer. The bride and groom had gone off to change into their going-away outfits and the vintage car, complete with the rope of old tin cans, was waiting at the back, ready to collect them from the front steps as soon as the fireworks show ended.

It was almost time for those fireworks. Penelope hadn't seen Rafe since that weirdly intense conversation under the tree. She hadn't even thought of him.

No. That wasn't entirely true. That persistent image of him was never far away from the back of her mind. And hadn't it got a bit closer right about the time she'd described herself as 'happily single' to that journalist?

And now he was here again, still wearing that hat, with a laptop bag slung over his shoulder. Right outside the kitchen door, when Penelope had hung up her apron and slipped back into the entrance hall so that she could go and find a place to watch the show.

'Ready?'

Words failed her. She could hear an echo of his voice from that earlier conversation.

I'll make sure you get the best spot to watch...

He'd kept his word. Again. She'd known she could trust him, hadn't she, when he'd turned up for that first meeting here?

Having that trust confirmed, on top of being drawn back into where she'd experienced the feeling that they were somehow connected on a secret level, was a mix so powerful it stole the breath, along with any words, from Penelope's body.

All she could do was nod.

A corner of his mouth lifted. 'Come on, then.' He held out his hand.

And Penelope took it. His grip was strong. Warm. A connection that was physical. Real, instead of the one that was probably purely only in her own imagination, but if she hadn't already been sideswiped by that visceral force, she would never have taken his hand.

Who in their right mind would start holding hands with a virtual stranger? One who had a 'bad boy' label that was practically a neon sign? What good girl would be so willing to follow him?

Not her. Not in this lifetime. She could almost hear her grandmother's voice. The mantra of her life. Her greatest fear.

'You'll end up just like your mother, if you're not very careful.'

How could it feel so good, then? Kind of like when she knew no one could see her and she could let loose and dance...

No one could see her now. Except Rafe. It was like being in one of her dreams, only she wasn't going to end up feeling that something wasn't fair because she didn't have to wake up any time soon. She had to almost skip a step or two to keep up with his long stride but then she tugged back on the pressure. Silly to feel fear at breaking such a little rule when she was already doing something so out of character but maybe it was symbolic.

'We can't go *upstairs.*'

'We have to. I need to get the best view of

the show. I've got people on the ground I can reach by radio if there's any problem but I have to be able to see.' He stepped over the thick red rope. 'It's okay. I'm not really breaking the sacred rules. I've cleared it with the owner.'

He sounded completely convincing. Maybe Penelope just wanted to believe him. Or perhaps the notion of going somewhere forbidden—in his company—was simply too enticing. She could probably blame that glass of champagne for giving in so readily. Or maybe it was because she was letting herself give in to the pulse of something too big to ignore. It might not look like it from the outside, but she was already dancing.

Up the stairs. Along a wide hallway. Past an open door that revealed a luxurious bathroom. Into...a *bedroom*? Yes, there was a four-poster bed that looked about as old as Loxbury Hall itself. It also looked huge and...dear Lord...irresistibly inviting. As if it was the exact destination she'd been hoping this man would lead her to.

Shocked, Penelope jerked her hand free of

Rafe's but he didn't seem to notice. He was open-ing French doors with the ease of knowing ex-actly where the latches were and then he glanced over his shoulder as they swung open.

'Come on, then. You won't see much in there.'

Out onto the flagged terrace, and the chill of the night air went some way to cooling the heat Penelope could feel in her cheeks. Hopefully, the heat deeper in her body would eventually cool enough to disappear as well.

Rafe checked in with his team by portable radio. Some were as close as it was safe to be to the action, with fire extinguishers available if something went seriously wrong. They would be working alongside him when the show was over, checking for any unexploded shells and then clearing up the rubbish of spent casings and roll-ing up the miles of cables to pack away with the rest of the gear.

For the next ten minutes, though, there was nothing to do but watch and see how the hard work of the last few days had come together. Rafe set up his laptop, activated the program that synched the music and effects and kept the radio channel open to have the ground team on standby for the countdown. Speakers had been set up along the terrace and the first notes of the song caught everybody's attention.

And then the first shells were fired and the sky filled with expanding, red hearts. The collective gasp from the crowd on the terrace below was loud enough to hear over the music for a split second before the next shell was detonated. The gasp from the woman in the silver dress beside him shouldn't have been loud enough to hear but, suddenly, it was Penelope's reaction that mattered more than anything else.

For the first time in his life in professional pyrotechnics, Rafe found he wasn't watching the sky but he could still gauge exactly what was happening. He could feel the resonance of the explosions in his bones and he could see the colours reflected on Penelope's face. He could see much

more than that as well. He could see the amaze-
ment, a hint of fear and the sheer thrill of it all.
He could feel what it was that had sucked him
into this profession so long ago with an intensity
that he hadn't realised had become blurred over
the years.

And he was loving it.

Penelope had seen fireworks before. Of course
she had. She'd always been a little frightened of
them. They were so loud. So unpredictable. Too
dangerous to really enjoy.

But she felt safer here. She was with the person
who was controlling the danger so she could let
go of that protective instinct that kept her ready to
run in an instant if necessary. She could let herself feel the boom of the explosions in her body
instead of bracing herself against them. She could
watch the unfurling of those astonishing colours
and shapes against the black sky. She could even
watch the new shells hurtling upwards with an

anticipation that was pure excitement about what was about to come.

She didn't want it to end. This was the ultimate finale to the biggest thing she had accomplished so far in her life. The wedding was done and dusted and it had been all she had hoped and dreamed it would be. She could let go of all that tension and bask in the satisfaction of hard work paying off.

It had to end, though. The music was beginning to fade. The huge red heart that looked as if it was floating in the middle of the lake came alive with the names of Clarrie and Blake appearing in white inside. The cheering from the crowd below was ecstatic and Penelope felt the same appreciation. Unthinking, she turned to Rafe to thank him but words were not enough in the wake of that emotional roller-coaster.

She stood on tiptoe and threw her arms around his neck.

'That was *amazing*. Thank you *so* much...'

* * *

The silver dress felt cool and slippery as his hands went automatically to the hips of the woman pressed against him but he could feel the warmth of her skin beneath the fabric.

This was the last thing Rafe had expected her to do.

He'd been reliving the passion of his job through watching her reaction to the show. Now, with this unexpected touch, he was reliving the excitement of touching a woman as if it were the first time ever. Was this the thing he'd lost? It was a sensation he hadn't even known he'd been pursuing so he couldn't have known it had been missing for so long, but surely it couldn't be real? If he kept on touching her, it would end up being the same as all the others. Or would it?

She drew back and she was smiling. Her eyes were dancing. She looked more alive than Rafe had ever seen her look.

She looked more beautiful than any woman had the right to look.

He had to find out if there was any more to this magic. If he kissed her, would it feel like the first time he'd ever kissed a woman he'd wanted more than his next breath?

He was going to *kiss* her.

Penelope had a single heartbeat to decide what she should do. No. There was no decision that needed to be made, was there? What she should do was pull away from this man. Apologise for being overly effusive in her thanks and turn and walk away.

It wasn't about what she should do. It was about what she *wanted* to do. And whether—for perhaps the first time in her life—she could allow herself to do exactly that. Were the things she had denied herself for ever *really* that bad? How would she know if she never even took a peek?

It was just a kiss but waiting for it to happen was like watching one of those shells hurtle into the darkness, knowing that it would explode and knowing how exciting it would be when it did.

The anticipation was unbearable. She *had* to

find out. Had to open the door to that secret place and step inside.

And the moment his lips touched hers, Penelope knew she was lost. Nothing had ever felt like this. Ever. The softness that spoke of complete control. Gentleness that was a glove covering unimagined, wild abandon.

Not a word was spoken but the look Rafe gave her when they finally stopped kissing asked a question that Penelope didn't want to answer. If she started thinking she would stop feeling and she'd never felt anything like this. It wasn't real—it had to be some weird alchemy of exhaustion and champagne, the thrill of the fireworks and the illicit thrill of an invitation to go somewhere so forbidden—but she knew it would never happen again and she couldn't resist the desire to keep it going just a little longer.

It was bliss. A stolen gift that might never be offered again.

Maybe it wasn't really so astonishing that this woman was capable of such passion. He'd seen her dancing, hadn't he? When she'd thought no one could see her. By a stroke of amazingly good fortune he was sharing that kind of space with her right now. Where nobody could see them. Where whatever got kept hidden so incredibly well was being allowed out to play. Maybe it was true that he wouldn't have chosen a woman like this in a million years but it was happening and he was going to make the most of every second.

Because the magic was still there. Growing stronger with every touch of skin on skin. It was like the first time. Completely new and different and…and just *more*. More than he'd ever discovered. More than he'd ever dreamed he could find.

He took Penelope to paradise and then leapt over the brink to join her. For a long minute then, all he could do was hold her as he fought to catch his breath and wait for his heart to stop pounding. As he tried—and failed—to make sense of the emotions tumbling through his head and heart.

Ecstasy and astonishment were mixed with something a lot less pleasant. Bewilderment, perhaps?

A sense of foreboding, even?

What the hell had just happened here?

And what on earth was going to happen next?

CHAPTER FOUR

THE HOUNDS OF HELL were chasing Penelope's car as she drove away from Loxbury Hall.

How awful had that been?

What an absolute, unmitigated train crash.

She'd felt the moment of impact and it had been, undoubtedly, the most shocking sensation of her life. There she'd been, lying in Rafe's arms, floating in a bubble of pure bliss—knowing that there was no place in the world that would ever feel this good.

This safe…

And then she'd heard it. Her grandmother's voice.

'What have you done, Penelope? Oh, dear Lord…it's your mother all over again…you wicked, wicked girl…'

Her worst fear. She'd spent her whole life resisting the temptation to give in to doing bad things and she'd just thrown it all away.

For *sex*… Lust. One of those deadly sins.

Her partner in crime hadn't helped.

'It was only sex, babe.' The look on his face hadn't helped. *'Okay, it was great sex but, hey… it's still no big deal. Don't get weird about it.'*

He had *no* idea how big a deal it was for her.

'It's not as if you have to worry about getting pregnant.'

As if using a condom made it okay. Maybe it did in the world he came from. The world she'd avoided for ever. Sex, drugs and rock 'n' roll.

Her mother's world.

Oh, she'd held it together for a while. Long enough to get her clothes on and retreat from that bedroom with some dignity at least. She'd gone to the downstairs cloakroom, relieved to find that the only people around were the clean-up crew and members of the band, who were still dismantling their sound system. She'd sat in a cubicle for a long time, hoping that the shaking would ease. That the memory of what it had been like in Rafe's arms would fade. Or that she would be able to reassign it as something as horrible as it should be instead of the most incredible experience she'd ever had.

One that she knew she might desperately want to have again.

No-o-o...

She couldn't be that girl. She wouldn't let herself.

Jack had taken one look at her face when she'd gone to the kitchen and simply hugged her.

'It's over, love. You get to go home and get some sleep. I'll finish up here. I've already packed the leftovers into your car. Those kids at the home are going to get a real treat for Sunday lunch this week.' He'd tightened his hug. 'You've done it. Awesome job. You can be very proud of yourself.'

Jack had no idea either, did he?

Somehow, she got home to the small apartment over the commercial kitchen that had been the base for her business for those first years. It was more of a test kitchen now and a back-up for when they needed things they didn't have the time or space to produce in the bigger kitchens that were Jack's domain, but it was full of memories and Penelope loved it with a passion. She transferred the containers of food to the cool room and then slammed the door to the street shut behind her and locked it, hoping to shut those hounds outside. But they followed her upstairs and she could see them circling her bed, waiting to move in for the kill.

One of them had her grandmother's face. Cold and disgusted. With sharp teeth ready to shave slivers of flesh from her bones with every accusation.

One of them had Rafe's face. With eyes that glowed with desire and a lolling tongue that promised pleasures she'd never dreamed of. It stopped and gave her what looked like a grin as she unzipped the silver dress and it felt like it was

Rafe's hands that were peeling the fabric from her body all over again.

Where did that heat come from? Coursing through her body like an electric shock that was delicious instead of painful?

Oh, yeah…it was the bad blood. Of course it was. How else could it move so fast and infuse every cell of her body?

Penelope balled the dress and threw it into the corner. So much for it being her trademark wedding outfit. She'd never be able to wear it again.

She'd never be able to sleep if she got into her bed either. The thought of lying there in the dark with those mental companions was unbearable. Even exhaustion wouldn't be enough protection.

Pyjamas were a good idea, though. Comfortable and comforting. Her current favourites were dark blue, with a pattern of silver moons and stars. A soft pair of knitted booties on her feet and Penelope was already feeling better. All she needed now was a cup of hot chocolate and the best thing about making that was that she could be in her kitchen and that was a comfort zone all of its own.

Or was it?

Encased in the upright, clear holder on the gleaming expanse of the stainless-steel bench was a recipe for cake. Red velvet cake. The cake she'd promised her grandmother she would provide for the dinner party tomorrow night to celebrate Grandad's birthday. No, make that tonight because Sunday had started hours and hours ago.

Before the fireworks. Before she'd blown up the foundations of her life by doing something so reckless she had no idea how to process any possible repercussions.

Easier not to think. To go on autopilot and do what she could do better than anyone. Opening cupboards, Penelope took out bowls and measuring cups and cake tins. She turned an oven on and went to the cool room and then the pantry to collect all the ingredients she would need.

Flour and cocoa. Unsalted butter and eggs

and buttermilk. Caster sugar and red paste food colouring. She could think about the icing later. Cream cheese for between the layers, of course, but the decoration on top would have to be spectacular to impress her grandmother. Maybe a whole bouquet of the delicate frosted roses that she was famous for.

It would take hours. Maybe so long she would have to leave her kitchen and go straight to her Sunday gig of making lunch for the residents of the Loxbury Children's Home. Another comfort zone.

How good was that?

It wasn't easy to identify the prickle of irritation because it had been a long time since Rafe Edwards had felt…guilty?

He didn't *do* guilt. He'd learned at a very young age that it was only justified if you hurt somebody intentionally and that was something else he never did. He refused to feel guilty for breaking rules that weren't going to damage anything bar the egos of people who thought they had the right to control what you did because they were more important. Better educated, or richer, or simply older.

The snort that escaped as he pulled his jeans back on was poignant. The age factor hadn't mattered a damn since he'd been sixteen. Nearly two decades since anyone had been able to make his life unbearable simply because they were old enough to have authority.

Back then, he'd get angry at being caught rather than feel guilty about what rule he'd broken. And maybe there was a smidge of anger to be found right now. Annoyance, for sure. Penelope had wanted it as much as he had, so why had she looked as if the bottom had fallen out of her world the moment her desire-sated eyes had focused again?

Yep. Annoyance had been why he'd baited her. Why he'd made no attempt to cover himself as he'd lain there with his arms hooked over the pillows behind him. Why he'd tried to dismiss what had happened as nothing important. Had he really said it was no big deal because she hadn't been in danger of getting pregnant?

It had been lucky he'd found that random condom in his pocket. Would either of them have been able to stop what had been happening by the time he'd gone looking? That was a scary thought. Unprotected sex was most certainly one of the rules that Rafe never broke because there was a real risk of someone getting hurt. A kid. Someone so vulnerable it was something he never even wanted to have to think about. Didn't want to have to remember…

Robot woman had returned as she'd scrambled into her clothes. Man, Penelope Collins was uptight. No wonder he'd avoided her type for ever. This aftertaste was unpleasant. A prickle under his skin that didn't feel like it was going to fade any time soon.

He didn't bother straightening the bed before he left the room. He owned the room now. And the bed, seeing as he'd bought the place fully furnished. It was the room he intended on using as his bedroom when he moved in but…dammit… would he ever be able to sleep in there without remembering that astonishing encounter?

And maybe that was where that irritation was coming from. Because he knew it was an encounter he was never going to get the chance to repeat.

Which was crazy because he didn't want to. Why would anybody want to if it left you feeling like this?

It was probably this disturbance to his well-being that made it take a second glance to recognise the man coming out of the ballroom when he got downstairs.

Or maybe it went deeper than that?

More guilt?

This was an old friend. One of the few good mates from the past that he hadn't spent nearly enough time with in recent years because his life had taken him in such a different direction. Such an upward trajectory.

This felt awkward. Was there a chance of being

seen as completely out of their league? Too important to hang out with them any more?

But there was relief to be found here, too, being drawn back into a part of his past he would never choose to abandon. A comfort zone like no other, and that was exactly what he needed right now.

And it appeared as if he was welcome, judging by the grin that split the man's face as he caught sight of Rafe.

'Hey, man… What the heck are you doin' here?'

'Scruff. Hey… Good to see you. Here, give me that.' Rafe took one of the huge bags that held part of the drum kit. 'I heard you and the boys. You're still sounding great.'

'Thanks, man. Still missing your sax riffs in some of those covers. Like that one of Adele's. If we'd known you were going to be here we would have hauled you on stage.'

The tone was light but there was a definite undercurrent there. Rafe hadn't been imagining the barrier he'd inadvertently erected with his neglect. Or maybe it was more to do with how successful he'd become. How rich…

'I was a bit busy. That fireworks show? Put that together myself. Haven't done the hands-on side of the business for years. It was fun.'

'It was awesome.' Scruff dumped the gear he was carrying beside the van parked on the driveway. He leaned against the vehicle to roll a cigarette and when it was done he offered it to Rafe.

'Nah, I'm good. Given it up, finally.'

'For real? Man…' Scruff lit the cigarette and took a long draw, eyeing Rafe over the smoke. The awkwardness was there again. He was different. Their relationship was different. 'Given up all your other vices, too?'

'Nah…' Rafe grinned. 'Some things are too good to give up.'

Like sex.

Scruff's guffaw and slap on the arm was enough to banish the awkwardness. And then other band members joined them and Scruff's delight in rediscovering a part of Rafe that he recognised was transmitted—unspoken—with no more than a glance.

Rafe was only too happy to take the rebukes of how long it had been. To apologise and tell them all how great it was to see them. Reunion time was just what he needed to banish that prickle.

The one that told him sex was never going to be anything like the same again.

Unless it was with Penelope Collins?

The enthusiasm of the other members of Diversion gained momentum as they finished packing their gear into the truck. 'Bout time you got yourself back where you belong. Party tomorrow night… No, make that *tonight*. You up for it?'

'You bet.'

Diversion's lead singer, Matt, grinned. 'We'd better send out some more invites. I can think of a few bods who'll want to see you again.'

Scruff snorted. 'Yeah…like the Twickenham twins.'

The sudden silence let him know that the boys were eyeing each other again. Still wondering how different he might be. It seemed important to diffuse that tension. To get into that comfort zone more wholeheartedly.

'Oh, no...' Rafe shook his head. 'They're still hanging around? Do they still dress up as cowgirls?'

'Sure do.' Scruff gave him a friendly punch on the arm. 'And they're gonna be mighty pleased to see you, cowboy.'

The prickle was fading already. With a bit of luck, normal service was about to be resumed. 'Bring it on. Just tell me where and when.'

The Loxbury Children's Home, otherwise known as Rainbow House, was on the opposite side of the city from Loxbury Hall and its style was just as different as the location. The building had no street appeal, with the haphazard extensions that had taken place over time and maintenance like painting that was well overdue, and the garden was littered with children's toys and a playground that had seen better days.

But it felt like home, and Maggie and Dave, the house parents, welcomed Penelope with the same enthusiasm as they'd done years ago—that very first time she'd turned up with the tentative offer of food left over from a catering event. The same age as her grandparents, Maggie and Dave were the parents Penelope had never had. The house, noisy with children and as messy and lived in as the garden, was so different from where she'd grown up that, for a long time, she'd felt guilty for enjoying it so much.

She'd gone back, though. Again and again. Maggie hadn't discovered for a long time that she actually cooked or baked things when there weren't enough leftovers to justify a weekly drop-off. When she did, she just gave Penelope one of those delicious, squishy hugs that large women seemed to be so good at.

'It's you we need more than free food, pet. Just come. Any time.'

It wasn't enough to just visit. Helping Maggie in the kitchen was the time she loved the best.

Cooking Sunday lunch with her favourite person in the world was a joy and what had become a weekly ritual was never broken.

She'd got to know a lot of the children now, too. The home offered respite care to disabled children and temporary accommodation to those in need of foster homes. There were the 'boomerang' kids who sadly bounced between foster homes for one reason or another and some long-term residents that places could never be found for. The home was always full. Of people. And love.

'Oh, my… Is that fillet steak?'

'It is. Jack over-catered for the wedding last night. It came with wilted asparagus and scalloped potatoes but I thought the kids might like chips and maybe peas.'

'Good idea. What a treat. Well, you know where the peeler is. Let's get on with it. Don't you have some special do at your folks' place tonight?'

'Mmm. Grandad's birthday. There's no rush,

though. I'm only doing dessert and I've made a cake. I don't need to turn up before seven-thirty.'

Maggie beamed. 'Just as well. The kids have got a play they want to put on for you after lunch. Have to warn you, though, it's a tad tedious.'

'Nothing on how tedious the dinner party's going to be. I'm almost thirty, Maggie, and I still get 'the look' if I use the wrong fork.'

Penelope rinsed a peeled potato under the tap and put it on the chopping board. She reached for another one from the sack and her damp hand came out covered in dirt. With a grimace, she turned the tap back on to clean it. Dusting the particles that had fallen onto her jeans only turned it into a smear but that didn't matter. She'd probably be rolling around on the floor, playing with one of the toddlers, before long. This was the only place she ever wore jeans and it was an illicit pleasure that fitted right in with not worrying about the mess or the noise. She'd just have to make sure she left enough time to shower and change when she went home to collect the cake.

'So, how was the wedding?' Maggie sounded excited. 'Did you know we could see the fireworks from here? A couple of the boys sneaked out to watch them and we didn't have the heart to tell them off for getting out of bed. They were so pretty.'

'Weren't they? I got the best view from upstairs at the hall.'

'Upstairs? I thought that was out of bounds?'

'Hmm. The guy doing the fireworks show had permission, apparently. He needed to be where he could see everything in case there was a problem.'

'And he took you upstairs, too?'

'Mmm.' Penelope concentrated on digging an eye out of the potato she was holding. 'Upstairs' was the least of the places Rafe had taken her last night but, no matter how much she loved and trusted Maggie, she couldn't tell her any of that.

She knew what happened when you did things that disappointed people.

They stopped loving you.

This time, when she picked up a new potato, the mud on her hand got transferred to her face as she stifled a sniff.

'You all right, pet?'

'Mmm.' Penelope forced a smile. 'Bit tired, that's all. It was a big night.'

'Of course it was.' Maggie dampened a corner of a tea towel and used it to wipe the grime off Penelope's cheek. 'Let's get this food on the table. You can have a wee snooze during the play later. It wouldn't go down too well if you fell asleep during dinner, would it? Your folks are going to want to hear all about everything that happened last night. They must be very proud of you. I certainly would be.'

Penelope's misty smile disguised a curl of dread. Imagine what would happen if she told her grandparents absolutely everything? But could she hide it well enough? Her grandmother had always had some kind of sixth sense about her even thinking about something she shouldn't and she'd always been able to weasel out a confession in the end, and a confession like this one would make the world as she knew it simply implode.

Oh, for heaven's sake. She hadn't been a child for a very long time. Wasn't it about time she stopped letting her grandparents make her feel like one?

It was one of the classic saxophone solos of all time. 'Baker Street' by Gerry Raffety. Rafe had first heard this song when he'd been an angry, disillusioned sixteen-year-old and it had touched something in his soul. When he'd learned that it had been released in 1978, the year he was born, the connection had been sealed. It was *his* song and he was going to learn to play the sax for no other reason than to own it completely.

And here he was, twenty years later, and he could close his eyes and play it as though the gleaming, gold instrument was an extension of his body and his voice. A mournful cry that had notes of rebellion and hope. So much a part of him that it didn't matter he hadn't had time to take the sax out of its case for months at a time. It was always there. Waiting for an opportunity that always came when it was needed most.

And, man, he'd needed it tonight, to exorcise that prickle that had refused to go away all day. Even walking the expanse of amazing gardens he could now call his own, as he'd collected the last of the charred cardboard that had enclosed the shells fired last night, hadn't been enough to soothe his soul. Or floating on his personal lake to retrieve the barge. Memories of the fireworks display that had been intended to celebrate his ownership of Loxbury Hall would be inextricably linked to other memories for ever.

Of a woman he'd never expected to meet and would never meet again.

But never mind. He could let it go now. 'Baker Street' had worked its magic again.

'That was awesome, dude.' Scruff had given his all to his drum accompaniment to the song. So had the guitarists and Diversion's keyboard player, Stefan. Now the beer was cold and there was plenty of comfortable old furniture in this disused warehouse that was the band's headquarters for practice and parties.

'As covers go, it's one of the best,' Stefan agreed. 'But it's time we wrote more of our own stuff.'

'Yeah…' Rafe took a long pull of his beer. 'You know what? I've been toying with the idea of setting up a recording company.'

Stefan's beer bottle halted halfway to his mouth. His jaw dropped and his gaze shifted from Rafe to Scruff, who shook his head. Was it his imagination or did the boys take a step further away from him? Okay, so he had more money than he used to have. More money than most people ever dreamed of, but it didn't change who he was, did it? Didn't change how much he loved these guys.

He shrugged, trying to make it less of a big deal. 'I could do with a new direction. Blowing things up is getting a bit old.'

So not true. But there had been a moment today, when memories of the fireworks and of Penelope had seemed so intertwined, that the idea of taking a break from his profession had seemed shockingly appealing.

'Get a whole new direction.' Scruff had recovered enough to grin. 'Join the band again. Come and experience the delights of playing covers at birthday parties and weddings. You too could learn every ABBA song in existence.'

The shout of laughter echoed in the warehouse rafters. He was forgiven for any differences and it felt great. A cute blonde with a cowboy hat on her bouncy curls and a tartan shirt that needed no buttons fastened between an impressive cleavage and the knot above a bare midriff came over to sit beside Rafe on the ancient couch. One of the Twickenham twins. He knew they'd been watching him closely all evening and their shyness had been uncharacteristic enough to make him feel the barriers were still there. Apparently, he'd just broken through the last of them.

'Nothing wrong with ABBA.' She pouted. 'It's great to dance to.'

'Yeah, baby…' Her identical sister came to sit on his other side. Somehow she moved so that his arm fell over her shoulder as if the movement had been intended. And maybe it had been. 'Let's dance…'

Lots of people were dancing already, over by the jukebox that had been the band's pride and joy when they'd discovered it more than a decade ago—when Rafe had been part of the newly formed band. A pall of smoke fog hung under the industrial lights and, judging by what he could smell, Rafe realised he could probably get high even if he didn't do stuff like that any more. The party was getting going and it was likely to still be going when dawn broke.

The thought brought a wave of weariness. Good grief…was he getting too old for this?

'Can't stay too long,' he heard himself saying. 'Got a board meeting first thing tomorrow. We're making a bid for New Year's Eve in London again this year. It's big.'

'Oh…*man*…' Scruff groaned. 'We just find you and you're gonna disappear on us again?'

'No way. I've bought a house around here now.'

'For real?'

'Yeah…' Rafe wiped some foam from above his top lip. 'Given my advancing years, I reckoned it was time to settle down somewhere.' Not that he was going to tell them where the house was yet. That would put him back to square one by intimidating them all with his wealth and success.

The laughter of some of his oldest friends was disquieting. Stefan couldn't stop.

'House first, then a wife and kids, huh?'

Rafe snorted. 'You know me better than that, Stef.'

The twins snuggled closer on both sides. 'You don't wanna do that, Rafey. A wife wouldn't want to play like we can.'

So true. The connotations of a wife brought up images of a controlling female. Someone who made sure she got everything precisely the way she wanted it.

Someone like Penelope Collins?

The soft curves of the twin cleavages that were close enough to touch and inviting enough to delight any man were curiously unappealing right now. There would be no surprises there. It might be nice but it would be old. Jaded, even, knowing that it was possible to feel like sex was brand-new and exciting again.

Rafe sighed. He had to get out of there. The prickle had come back to haunt him.

'You're not the only one with something big coming up,' Scruff said into the silence that fell. 'We're gonna be a headline act at the festival next month.'

'The Loxbury music festival?' Rafe whistled. 'Respect, man.' Then he frowned. 'I thought they'd wound that gig up years ago. Too much competition from the bigger ones like Glastonbury.'

'They did. It's been nearly ten years but this

year is the thirtieth anniversary. The powers that be decided it would be a great blast from the past and put little ol' Loxbury back on the map.'

'Sounds fun. You'll get to play some of your own stuff.'

'You could be in on it, mate. You'd love what we're doing these days. Kind of Pink Floyd meets Meatloaf.'

The other band members groaned and a general argument broke out as they tried to define their style.

One of the twins slid her arm around Rafe's neck. 'There's going to be a big spread in one of the music mags. That's Julie over there. She's a journo and she's going to be doing the story. Did you know a girl died at the very first festival?'

'No… Really?'

'That's not true,' the other twin said. 'She collapsed at the festival. She didn't die until a couple of days later. It was a drug overdose.' She raised her voice. 'Isn't that right, Julie?'

'That's not great publicity to rake up before this year's event.'

'There's a much better story.' Julie had come over to perch on the end of the couch. 'There's Baby X.'

'Who the heck is Baby X?'

'The baby that got found under a bush when they were packing up. A little girl. They reckoned she was only a few days old.'

'She'll be nearly thirty now, then.' The twins both shuddered. 'That's old.'

'Not as old as me.' But Rafe was barely listening any more. Penelope's words were echoing in his head.

My mother abandoned me as a baby and then died. I have no idea who my father is.

Holy heck… Was it possible that *she* was Baby X?

The idea that the renewed curiosity of this journalist could expose a personal history that had to be painful was disturbing.

He should warn Penelope. Just in case.

Not his business, he told himself firmly. And that would mean he'd have to see her again and that was the last thing he wanted.

He drained his beer and then stood up, extracting himself with difficulty from the clutches of the twins. If he was going to believe what he was telling himself, he needed to get a lot more convincing.

He had to get out of there. He wasn't having fun any more.

The resolution to keep an adult poise along with any secrets she might wish to keep lasted all the way to the elegant old house in one of Loxbury's best suburbs. Her shower might have washed away the effects of so many sticky fingers but the glow of the cuddles and laughter was still with her. Her jeans were in the washing machine and she knew her new outfit would meet with approval. A well-fitted skirt, silk blouse and tailored jacket. There were no runs in her tights and she'd even remembered to wear the pearls that had been a twenty-first birthday gift from her grandparents, along with the start-up loan to start her small bakery.

A loan that was about to be paid off in full. Another step to total independence. She was an adult, she reminded herself again as she climbed the steps carefully in her high heels. The same shoes she'd worn the day she'd gone to the office of All Light on the Night. The same shoes that Rafe had tugged off her feet last night shortly after he'd unzipped that silver dress…

Penelope needed to take a deep, steadying breath before she rang the bell. She had a key to the kitchen door but rarely used it. By implicit agreement, being granted admission to the house she'd grown up in was the 'right' thing to do.

As was the kiss on her grandmother's cheek that barely brushed the skin and, instantly, she was aware of the child still hidden deep inside. Having skinny arms peeled away from their target with a grip strong enough to hurt.

'Don't hug me, Penelope. If there's anything I detest, it's being hugged.'

'How are you, Mother?'

'Fabulous, darling. And you?' She didn't wait for a response. 'Oh, is that the cake? Do let me see. I do hope it's Madeira.'

'Red velvet.'

'Oh…' The sound would have seemed like delighted surprise to somebody who didn't know Louise Collins. Penelope could hear the undertone of disapproval and it took her back instantly to the countless times she had tried so hard to win affection instead of simply acceptance. Why did it still matter? You'd think she would have given up long before this but somehow, beneath everything, she loved her grandmother with the kind of heartfelt bond she'd had as a tiny child, holding her arms up for a cuddle.

It was a relief that the beat of silence was broken by the arrival of another figure in the entranceway. Maybe this was why she'd never been able to let go. Why it still mattered so much.

'Grandad! Happy birthday…' This time the kiss was real and it went with a hug. A retired and well-respected detective inspector with the Loxbury police force, the happiest times of Penelope's childhood had been the rare times alone with her grandfather. Being hugged. Being told that she was loved. Being taken fishing, or on a secret expedition to buy a gift for her grandmother.

The grandmother who'd never allowed the real relationship to be acknowledged aloud.

'For goodness' sake, Penelope. I was only forty-three when you turned up on our doorstep. Far too young to be called a grandmother.'

'I'll take the cake into the kitchen, shall I?'

'Let me have a peek.' Douglas Collins lifted the lid of the box. 'Louise, look at these roses. Aren't they fabulous?'

'Mmm.' Louise closed the box again. 'Don't stay nattering to Rita in the kitchen, Penelope. The champagne's already been poured in the drawing room.'

Rita always made you remember the old adage

of 'never trust a thin cook'. Even bigger than Maggie, her hugs were just as good and her praise of the cake meant the most.

'Red velvet? Oh…I can't wait to taste it. Make sure there's some left over.'

'You should get the first piece, Rita. You're the one who taught me to bake in the first place.'

'Never taught you to do them fancy roses. I always said you were a clever girl.'

'I only *felt* clever when I was in here. It's no wonder I ended up being a baker, is it?'

'You're a sight more than that now. How did the wedding go?'

'It was fabulous. As soon as the magazines come out with the pictures, I'll bring some round for you.' The tinkle of a bell sounded from well beyond the kitchen and the glance they exchanged was conspiratorial. Penelope grinned. 'I'll pick a time when the olds are out and we can have a cuppa and a proper natter then.'

'I'd love that, sweet. You go and have them bub-

bles and enjoy your family time now. Go on…
scoot before her ladyship rings that bell again.'

How ironic was it that 'family time' had already been had today. First with Maggie and
Dave and then with Rita in the refuge of her
childhood.

The messy places that were always warm and
smelled of food.

The drawing room should have been overly
warm thanks to the unnecessary coals glowing
in the enormous fireplace, but somehow the per-
fection of every precisely placed object and the
atmosphere of a formal visit created a chill. Tast-
ing the champagne as they toasted the birthday
didn't help either, because it made Penelope remember the taste in her mouth last night, when
she'd emerged from the kitchen to take Rafe's
hand and let him lead her upstairs.

The spiral of sensation in her belly at the memory couldn't have been less appropriate in this
setting. Closing her eyes with a silent prayer, Penelope took another gulp.

'You look tired.' Her grandmother's clipped tones made it sound like she was excusing her lack of manners in drinking too fast. 'I hope you got some rest today instead of playing cook at that orphanage place.'

'Orphanages don't exist any more, Mother. Not like they used to.'

'I know that, Penelope.'

Of course she did. She'd probably gone searching for one as an alternative to doing the right thing and claiming their baby granddaughter.

'Charity work is to be commended, Louise. You know that better than anyone.' That was Grandad in a nutshell. Trying to keep the peace and protect his beloved wife at the same time. He'd always done that. Like the way he'd explained away some of the endless punishments and putdowns meted out by Louise.

She's only trying to keep you safe, sweetheart. We know what it's like to lose a precious little girl.

And now it was her turn to be soothed. 'Good

on you, Penelope, if you went and helped when you were tired.'

'I wouldn't call it charity.' Oh, help. Why was she contradicting everything being said? She took another gulp of champagne and found, to her horror, that she'd drained her glass.

'Of course it's charity. Those children are riff-raff that nobody wants. With no-good parents that probably spend all their money on cigarettes and alcohol and have no idea how to set boundaries for themselves, let alone their offspring.'

'Mmm...' Penelope was heading for the ice bucket that held the champagne bottle. 'Bad blood,' she murmured.

'Exactly.'

The long pause was enough for the silent statement that was as familiar as a broken record.

You can't help having bad blood. You just have to fight against it. Otherwise you know what can happen.

Yep. Penelope knew.

She'd end up just like her mother.

Funny that the ice bucket was on the occasional table right beside the fireplace. And that family photos were positioned artfully on the top of the mantelpiece. There was Penelope in a stiff, ruffled dress, aged about three, clutching a teddy bear that the photographer had had available in his studio.

A not dissimilar professional portrait of another small girl was to one side of an equally posed portrait of her grandparents' wedding. This girl had the same blonde hair as Penelope but her skin was much paler and her eyes were blue. One of the few pictures of her mother, Charlotte—before she'd gone off the rails so badly.

It wasn't that the Collins blood was bad, of course. Charlotte had been led astray by the person who'd really had it. The unknown father whose genes had overridden her mother's to give Penelope her brown eyes and more olive skin. A permanent reminder to her grandparents of the man who'd destroyed their perfect little family.

Louise Collins rose gracefully to her feet. 'I'll

go and let Rita know we're ready for the soup. Come through to the dining room, Penelope.'

'On my way.' Or she would be, when she'd filled her glass again. Heaven knew, she needed some assistance to get through the next hour or so of conversation without causing real trouble. Falling out with her grandmother any more than she had already this evening would only distress Grandad.

The worst thing about it all was that she had just learned what it was like when you lost the fight with the 'bad blood'.

And it was a lot more fun than she was having right now.

CHAPTER FIVE

NEARLY THREE WEEKS.

It should have been plenty of time to put any thoughts of Penelope Collins to bed—so to speak.

No…wrong choice of expression. Rafe Edwards closed his eyes for a moment to try and quell that surge of sensation that was inevitable whenever thoughts of Penelope and beds collided.

Maybe this was a mistake. He eyed the old building in the heart of Loxbury's industrial area with deep suspicion. Why had it even occurred to him that it might be a *good* idea?

Karma?

The amusement that was inherent?

Or was he being pulled along by some cosmic force he couldn't resist?

Fate.

With a dismissive snort, Rafe slammed the door of his four-by-four behind him. He didn't believe in any of that kind of rubbish. You made your own fate unless you were rendered powerless by youth or natural disaster or something. And success was sweet when it was earned.

Perhaps that was why he had grudging respect for Penny.

Oops...*Penelope.*

From the outside they were total opposites but there was a driving force at a deeper level that they both shared. Judging by the magazine and newspaper coverage of that wedding, Penelope was now poised for extraordinary success and she'd earned it. For whatever reason, she was carving her own niche in the world and she was doing it exceptionally well.

Plus...

Rafe rapped on the iron door that was the only entrance the building had to the street. No doubt there was a sparkling commercial kitchen behind the door with a team of loyal employees who could do their jobs with the kind of military precision Ms Collins would demand. Given how late in the day it was, however, it would be disappointing if the door was opened by someone other than the woman he'd come to see.

He wasn't disappointed. It was Penelope who opened the door.

'G'dday…' Rafe let his grin build slowly. 'I think you might owe me a favour.'

Oh…*no*…

She'd assumed it was Jack, who'd said he might drop in the new menus he was working on. She would never have opened the door otherwise. Not when she was wearing her pyjamas and slipper socks, with her hair hanging loose down her back. Funny how she'd never thought it might be a problem, with the only windows facing the street being on the next level where her apartment was.

How stupid was it not to have bothered using the peephole in the door? Not only stupid, but dangerous. It could have been anyone demanding entrance. A drug addict, for instance. Or an axe murderer.

Or…or…*Rafe*…

And he was calling in a favour?

He was still grinning at her. 'I realise you're probably beating off clients after getting so famous.'

'I… Ah…' Yes. Potential bookings were pouring in in the wake of the Bingham-Summers wedding. And part of that success had been down to its glorious finale with the fireworks. And, yes… Rafe had made that happen when he hadn't had the slightest obligation to, so she did owe him a favour.

But what on earth could he want from her?

The thought of what she might *want* him to want from her was enough to make her knees feel distinctly wobbly and that was more than a little disturbing. She'd got past that lapse of character. It had been weeks ago. Her life was back on track. More than back on track. Penelope tried to pretend that she was wearing her suit and high heels. That her hair was immaculate. She straightened her back.

'The thing is, All Light on the Night is booked to blow up a car on a movie set the day after tomorrow but the gig's about to be postponed, which doesn't suit us at all.'

Penelope had no idea where this conversation was going so she simply stared at him. Which was possibly a mistake. Beneath that battered hat she could see the tousled hair that her treacherous fingers remembered burying themselves in and below that there was a glint in those dark eyes that made her think he was finding this amusing. More than that—he was quite confident that she might find it amusing, too. Because he knew what she liked and he was more than able to deliver?

Penelope dragged her gaze away from his eyes. Dropped them to his mouth. Now, that really was a mistake. Staring at his lips, she could almost feel her body softening. Leaning towards him. Hastily, she straightened again.

'Sorry, what was that?'

'The catering company. It went on a forty-eight-hour strike today. Something to do with the union. Your workforce doesn't belong to a union, does it?'

'Um…not that I know of.' They'd started with only herself and Jack. Other employees had come via word of mouth and the company had grown slowly. They were like a family and there'd never been a hint of an industrial dispute.

'So you could take on the job? It's not huge. Just an afternoon and there'd only be a couple of dozen people to cater for, but film crews do like to eat and they like the food to be on tap. Catering for a movie set could be a whole new line of business for you. Could be a win-win situation for both of us, even.'

'In a couple of days?' Initial shock gave way—surprisingly—to a flicker of amusement at the way he was using the exact turn of phrase she'd tried on him in his office that day. Had he remembered that visit in the same kind of detail she had? 'We usually book that kind of job well in advance. *Months* in advance sometimes.' Her lips twitched. 'I could certainly give you a list of other companies that might be able to help.'

Rafe put an elbow up to lean against the door-frame. It pulled the front of his leather jacket further apart and tightened the black T-shirt across his chest. 'But I don't want another company,' he said. 'I have to have the best and…and I suspect that might be *you*.'

Penelope swallowed hard. She knew what was under that T-shirt. That smooth skin with just enough chest hair to make it ultimately masculine. Flat discs of male nipples that tasted like honey…

Taste. Yes. He was talking about food, she reminded herself desperately. *Food…*

'Have…have you got any idea what's involved with setting up a commercial catering event?'

'Nope.' He quirked an eyebrow and tilted his

head. He could probably see into the huge kitchen area behind her anyway so did he really have to lean closer like that? Was he waiting for an invitation to come inside and discuss it?

Not going to happen. It was no help trying to channel thoughts of being dressed in something appropriate. She was in her pyjamas, for heaven's sake. At seven-thirty p.m. Any moment now and she might die of embarrassment.

'There's meetings to be had with the client.' Her tone was more clipped than she had intended. 'Menus and budgets and so forth to be discussed.'

'The budget won't be an issue.'

Another turn of phrase she'd used herself that day in his office. When she'd been desperately trying to persuade him to help her. Impossible not to remember that wave of hope when he'd said he might be able to do it himself.

She could do the same for him. Already, a part of her brain was going at full speed. Mini amosas and spring rolls perhaps—with dipping sauces of tamarind and chili. Bite-sized pies.

Sandwiches and slices. It wouldn't be that hard. If she put in a few hours in her kitchen tonight, she could get all the planning and a lot of the prep done. She could use the old truck parked out the back that had been her first vehicle for getting catered food to where it was needed.

It might even be fun. A reminder of her first steps to independence and how far she'd come.

'Will you be there?' The query popped out before she could prevent it. What did it matter?

'Oh, yeah...' That wicked grin was back. 'I love blowing things up. Wouldn't miss it. The real question is...' The grin faded and there was something serious about his face now. 'Will *you* be there?'

That flicker of something behind the amusement told her that he wanted her to be there, but was it only about the food?

Penelope couldn't identify the mix of emotions coming at her but it was obvious they were stemming from that place she thought she'd slammed the door on. It would be a struggle to try and contain them and…and maybe it wouldn't be right.

Even her grandmother would tell her that she had an obligation to return a favour.

'Okay.' She tried to make it sound like it wasn't a big deal. 'Give me the details and I'll see what I can do.'

'How 'bout I email them through to you tomorrow?' He tugged on the brim of his hat and she could swear he was smirking as he turned away. 'Don't want to be keeping you up or anything.'

The flood of colour heated her cheeks so much that Penelope had to lean against the cool iron door after she swung it closed. Nobody knew that she liked to wear her pyjamas in the evenings when she wanted to relax. It would have been okay for Jack to find out but…*Rafe*?

Good grief. Penelope tried to think of something to make her feel less humiliated and finally it came to her.

At least he hadn't caught her dancing.

The thought was enough to get her moving. She

needed to check supplies in the cold room and the freezers and start making a plan. The way to get over this humiliation was crystal clear. Even if it was only for an afternoon, this was going to be the best damned catering this movie company—and the visiting pyrotechnicians—had ever experienced.

Man, the food was good.

Rafe wasn't the only person on set to keep drifting back to the food truck and the long table set out beside it. Those delicious little triangles of crispy filo pastry filled with potato and peas in a blend of Indian flavours, along with that dark, fruity sauce, were irresistible. Just as well the platter kept getting replenished and he'd arrived just in time to get them at their hottest.

Just in time for Penelope to be putting the platter on the table, in fact.

'Definitely my favourite,' he told her. 'Good job.'

It was more than a good job. She'd not only

made it possible for everyone to keep to schedule, there were a lot of people saying they'd never been so well fed on set. His praise brought out a rather endearing shyness in Penelope. She ducked her head and wiped her hands on her apron.

'Samosas are always popular. Try the spring rolls, too, before they run out. These guys sure do like to eat, don't they?'

She wasn't meeting his gaze. Maybe that shyness was left over from the other night when he'd caught her wearing her PJs.

And hadn't that been totally unexpected? About as strange as seeing this uptight woman dancing in the middle of his maze. There were layers to Penelope Collins that just didn't fit. It wasn't the things that were opposite to him that intrigued him. It was the opposites that were in the same person. Did she actually know who she really was herself?

Not that he was going to embarrass her by mentioning the PJs or anything. She'd returned his favour and he was grateful. And that would be the end of it.

'Won't be for much longer. We're all set for the filming and we only get one take.'

'Really? They seem to have been filming the same scene for ages.'

Rafe glanced behind him. They were in a disused quarry and the road had already been used for the sequence of the car rolling off the road.

'That was the hero getting the girl out of the car. I think they've nailed it now. He gets to help her run away from it next and when they hit a certain point is when we blow up the car. My boys are just getting the explosives rigged. It'll look like they're close enough to be in danger but they won't be, of course. All smoke and mirrors but we need the shot of them with the explosion happening behind them and that'll be it for the day.' He glanced upwards. 'Which is just as well. Those thunderclouds are perfect for a dramatic background but nobody wants their expensive camera gear out in the rain.'

'Is it going to be really loud?'

'Hope so. Should be spectacular, too, but you won't see much from here. Want to come where you will be able to get a good view?'

What was he thinking? The flash in her eyes told him she remembered agreeing to that once before and she hadn't forgotten where they'd ended up. The way her pupils dilated suggested that it had been an experience she wouldn't be entirely averse to repeating.

This was supposed to be the end of their association. Favours given and returned but, heaven help him, Rafe felt a distinct stirring of a very similar desire.

'No.' The vigorous shake of her head looked like she was trying to persuade herself. 'I can't. I'm here to do a job.'

'You can just leave it all on the table. Everybody's going to be busy for a while, believe me. Have you ever seen a car being blown up before?'

'N-no...'

'There you go, then. An opportunity missed is an opportunity wasted.'

It was more than a bit of a puzzle why he was trying to persuade her. It was even more of a puzzle why he felt so good when she discarded her apron and followed him to a point well out of shot to one side of the set. He used his radio to check in.

'You all set, Gav? Can you see the point they have to cross before you hit the switch?'

'All good to go, boss.' The radio crackled loudly. 'Reception's a bit crap. …are you?'

'Other side. Raise a flag if you need me.'

'Roger…' The blast of static made him turn the volume down. 'Something to do with the quarry walls, I guess. They won't need me. I don't usually even come to gigs like this any more.'

Oops. Why had he let that slip? Not that Penelope seemed to notice. She was watching the actors being positioned for the take. Make-up artists were touching up the blood and grime the accident and extrication had created. Cameras were being shifted to capture the scene from all angles. The director was near a screen set up for him to watch the take on the camera filming the central action and the guy holding the clipboard moved in front, ready for the command to begin the take.

'Places, please,' someone shouted. 'Picture is up.'

This was a lot more exciting than Penelope had expected it to be. So many people who seemed to know exactly what they were doing. There were cameras on tripods, others being held, one even on top of a huge ladder that looked rather too close to the car, which must be stuffed full of explosives by now. A sound technician, with his long hair in a ponytail, was wearing head-phones and holding a microphone that looked like a fluffy broomstick. The actors were wait-ing, right beside the car, for the signal to start running.

'That door's going to blow off first,' Rafe said,

his tone satisfied. 'With a bit of luck it'll really get some air at about the same time both ends of the car explode.'

'I hope they're far enough away by then.' Penelope kept her voice down, although they were probably far enough away for it not to matter if they talked.

'See where that camera on the tracks is? There's a white mark on the ground well in front of that. When the actors step across that, it's the signal to throw the switch. There's no chance of them getting hit by anything big.' He shielded his eyes with his hand as he stared across the open ground between them and the car. 'There might not be that many rules I regard as sacred but safety is top of the list.'

Penelope's gaze swerved to his face. The anticipation of waiting for a huge explosion was making her feel both scared and excited. The notion that even her safety was important to Rafe did something weird and, for a heartbeat, it felt like she was falling.

But it also felt like she *was* safe.

Rafe was right beside her. He would catch her before she could get hurt.

As if he felt the intensity of her gaze, his head turned and that weird feeling kicked up several notches. A split second before the eye contact could get seriously significant, however, a loud clap of wood on wood and the shout of 'Action' distracted them both.

Game on.

The actors were doing a good job of making it look like a panicked struggle to get away from the crashed vehicle as flames flickered behind them. The girl was only semi-conscious, blood dripping down her face, and the guy was holding her upright and pleading with her to try and go faster.

Penelope could feel Rafe's tension beside her. He had his hand shielding his eyes again and was looking beyond the actors, who were getting closer to the white mark.

The vehement curse that erupted from his lips made her jump.

'What's wrong?'

But Rafe ignored her. He grabbed his radio and pressed the button.

'Gav? Abort...abort... There's a bloody *kid* behind the car.'

The only sound in return was a burst of static. With another curse, Rafe took off, taking a direct line from where they stood to the side towards the car.

The car that was about to explode...

'Oh, my God...' Penelope couldn't breathe. She stood there, with her hands pressed to her mouth. Should she do something? Run towards the director and shout for help, maybe?

But Rafe was almost at the car now and surely someone had seen what was happening?

Her feet wouldn't move in any case. She'd never felt so scared in her life. With her heart in her mouth she watched Rafe reach the car. He vanished for a moment behind it and then reappeared—a small figure in his arms and half over one shoulder. Incredibly, he seemed to run even faster with his burden. Off to the side and well away from the line the actors had taken.

Were still taking.

In absolute horror, Penelope's gaze swung back to see them cross the white mark and then the first explosion made her cry out with shock. From the corner of her eye she could see the door of the car spiral into the air just the way Rafe had said it would, but she wasn't watching. Another explosion—even louder—and the car was a fireball. Big, black clouds of smoke spread out and she couldn't see Rafe any longer.

Couldn't think about how close he'd been to that explosion and that something terrible had just happened.

She was safe but—dear Lord—she didn't *want* to be safe in that moment. She wanted to be with Rafe. To know that *he* was safe…

And suddenly there he was. Emerging from the

cloud of smoke, still well to the side of the set. Still with the child in his arms.

There was no missing what was happening now. All hell broke loose, with people running and shouting, coming towards Penelope from one side as Rafe came from the other. She was right in the middle as they met.

'What the hell's going on?' The director sounded furious. 'What in God's name is that kid doing here? Where'd he come from?'

'He was hiding behind the car.' The director's fury was nothing on what Penelope could hear in Rafe's voice. His face was grimy from the smoke and his features could have been carved out of stone as he put the boy down on his feet.

And Penelope had never seen a man look more compelling. Then her gaze shifted to the boy and she was shocked all over again. She'd seen this child before.

'Billy?' The name escaped in a whisper that no one heard but the boy's gaze flew to meet hers

and she could see the terror of a child who knew he was in serious trouble.

A man in a fluorescent vest, holding a radio, looked as white as a sheet.

'Tried to call you to abort firing, Gav,' Rafe snapped. 'Reception was zilch.'

'We had security in place. Nobody got into the quarry without a pass.'

'He was with me.' Penelope cleared her throat as every face swung towards her, including Rafe's. 'In the food truck. I'm sorry...' She turned towards the boy. 'You knew you were supposed to stay inside, didn't you, Billy? What were you *thinking*?'

Billy hung his head and said nothing but Penelope could see the tremor in his shoulders. He was trying very hard not to cry.

Lifting her gaze, she found Rafe glaring at her with an intensity that made her mouth go dry. He knew she was lying.

'He was thinking he might want to get himself killed,' Rafe said quietly. 'He very nearly succeeded.'

'But he didn't.' Penelope gulped in a new breath. 'Thanks to you.'

'I'll have to file an incident report,' the director said, his anger still lacing every word. 'I should call the police. The kid was trespassing.'

'No.' Penelope took a step towards the boy and put her arm around his shoulders. 'Please, don't call the police. I take full responsibility. It's not Billy's fault. It's mine. I should have stayed in the truck with him.'

'You shouldn't have brought him on set in the first place.'

'I know. I'm sorry. But he knew a car was going to get blown up and it was too exciting an opportunity to miss.' She flicked a glance at Rafe. Would he hear the unspoken plea to get him on side by repeating the words he'd used to persuade her?

As if to underline her plea, a distant clap of thunder unrolled itself beneath boiling clouds.

And then raindrops began to fall. Heavy and instantly wetting.

The director groaned. 'This is all we need.'

'Shall we start packing up, chief?' someone asked.

There was a moment of hesitation in which it felt like everyone was holding their breath.

'I'll deal with it,' Penelope offered. 'I'll see that Billy gets the punishment he deserves.'

'I think that's *my* call.' Rafe's voice had a dangerous edge. 'Don't you?'

The heat of his glare was too intense to meet but Penelope nodded. So did Billy.

'Fine.' The director held both hands up in surrender. 'It's your safety regulations that got breached. And it was you that brought this flaky caterer on set. You deal with it.' He turned away, making a signal that had the crew racing to start getting equipment out of the rain, but he had a parting shot for Rafe. 'You have no idea how lucky you are that no harm was done. You'd be out of the movie business for good if it had.' He shook his head. 'You're also lucky that your heroics didn't show up on screen or we'd have to be reshooting and you'd be paying for it, mate.'

The last person to leave was Gav.

'I'll pack down and clear the site,' he said. He cast a curious glance at Penelope and Billy. 'Guess you'll be busy for a while.'

The rain was coming down steadily now. The kid was visibly shivering in his inadequate clothing and the look on his face was sullen enough to suggest he was used to getting into trouble.

Rafe saw the way Penelope drew him closer. For a moment the kid resisted but then he slumped as if totally defeated. He wasn't looking at either of the adults beside him but Penelope was looking and she didn't look at all defeated. Her chin was up and she looked ready to go into battle. What was it with this kid? How on earth did Penelope even know his name?

'Want to tell me what this is all about?' Rafe wasn't about to move and any sympathy for how uncomfortable either of these people felt hadn't kicked in yet. 'There's no way this kid was in your truck when you got here.'

'The kid has a name,' Penelope shot back. 'It's Billy.'

'How did you get anywhere near that car, Billy?'

He got no response.

'He didn't know you were going to blow it up. He—'

'Billy's not a puppet,' Rafe snapped. 'Stop talking for him.'

Penelope's mouth opened and closed. She glared at Rafe.

'Billy? Or is your real name William?'

A small sound from Penelope told him that she got the reference to her own name preference. The kid also made a sound.

'What was that?'

'Billy. Only rich kids get called William.'

'And how do you know Penelope?'

'I don't.'

That made sense. Billy looked like a street kid.

Like he'd looked about the same age? Rafe pushed the thought away. He didn't want to go there.

'How does she know your name, then?'

'Dunno.' Billy kicked at the ground with a shoe that had a hole over his big toe.

'I help out at a local children's home.' Penelope's tone was clipped, as if she expected to get reprimanded for speaking again. 'I've met Billy there a couple of times in the last few years when things haven't been so good at home.'

That also made sense. A bit of charity work on the side would fit right in with the image that Ms Collins presented to the world. The image that hid the person she really was?

Rafe stifled an inward sigh. 'So, is that why you sneaked into the quarry? Trying to find a place away from home?'

'I was playing, that's all.' The first direct look Rafe received was one of deep mistrust. 'I saw them doing stuff to the car and I wanted a closer look. You didn't have to come and get me. It was none of your business, man.'

Whoa…did this kid know that he'd almost got killed and didn't care? The anger was still there. In spades.

'You don't get to make decisions like that,' he told Billy. 'Not at your age.'

An echo of something unpleasant rippled through him. People making decisions for him because he was too young. People making rules. Making things worse.

But this was about safety. Keeping a kid alive long enough for him to get old enough to make his own decisions—stupid or otherwise.

'I'm taking you home,' he said. 'I want a word with your parents.'

'No *way*…' Billy ducked under Penelope's arm and took off. If the ground hadn't become slippery already from the rain, he might have made it, but Rafe grabbed him as he got back to his feet. And he held on.

'Fine. If you don't want to go home, we'll go and have a chat to the cops.'

'No.' Penelope looked horrified. 'Don't you think he's got enough to deal with, without getting more of a police record at his age?'

More of a police record? Good grief.

'I'll take him to Maggie and Dave. They'll know what to do.'

'Who the heck are Maggie and Dave?'

'They run Rainbow House—the children's home. They're the best people I know.'

There was passion in her voice. Something warm and fierce that made Rafe take another look at her face. At her eyes that were huge and… vulnerable?

'And how do you think you're going to get him to this home? In the back of your truck that he could jump out of at the first set of traffic lights?' The tug on his arm confirmed his suspicions so he tightened his grip.

Penelope faced Billy. 'You've got a choice,' she said. 'You can either come with me and see Maggie and Dave or go to the police station. What'll it be?'

Billy spat on the ground to show his disgust. 'You can't make me go anywhere.'

'Wanna bet?' Rafe was ready to move. It was easy to take the kid with him. 'Let's go back to your truck, Penelope. We can call the police from there.'

'No.' Billy kicked Rafe's ankle. He stopped and took hold of the boy's other arm as well, bodily lifting him so that he could see his face.

'That's enough of that, d'you hear me? We're trying to *help* you.'

'That's what they all say.' There was a desperation in Billy's voice that was close to a sob as he struggled for freedom. 'And they don't *help.* They just make everything worse...'

Oh, man... This was like looking into some weird mirror that went back through time.

'Not Maggie and Dave...' Penelope had come closer. Close enough to be touching Rafe's shoulder. Was it just the rain or did she have tears running down her cheeks? 'They can help, Billy. I know they can.'

'Then that's where we'll go.'

'We?'

'I'm coming with you.' He couldn't help his exasperated tone. 'You can't do this by yourself.'

Which was a damned shame because Rafe could do without a trip to some home for problem kids. Could do without the weird flashbacks, thanks very much. But he'd only get more of them if he left this unresolved, wouldn't he?

And this was supposed to be the end of his association with Penelope Collins. It would be a shame to leave it on such a sour note.

'Let's get going,' he growled, as another clap of thunder sounded overhead. 'Before we all catch pneumonia.'

CHAPTER SIX

IF PENELOPE HAD been a frightened child with a home she was scared to go back to, then Rainbow House was exactly the place she'd want to be. She knew she was doing the right thing here, but the vibes from the two males in the front seat of her little food truck told her they didn't share her conviction.

Penelope was driving and Billy was sandwiched between the two adults to prevent any attempt to escape. A sideways glance as they neared their destination revealed remarkably similar expressions on their faces. It could have been a cute 'father and son' type of moment, except that the expressions were sullen. They were both being forced to do something that ran deeply against the grain. Being punished.

Her heart squeezed and sent out a pang of… what? Sympathy? There was something more than the expressions that was similar. Had Rafe been a kid who had broken every rule in the book to get some attention? He still broke rules—look at the total lack of appreciation for the stated boundaries at Loxbury Hall. Not that he needed to do anything to attract attention now. He was the most gorgeous man she'd ever seen. He was clever and passionate about his work. And he'd just risked his life to save a child.

The memory of the wave of emotion when she'd seen him emerge from the smoke unharmed made her grip the steering-wheel tightly. It gave her an odd prickly sensation behind her eyes, as though she was about to cry—which was disturbing because she had learned not to cry a long time ago.

'Don't cry, for heaven's sake, Penelope. The only difference it makes is that your face gets ugly.'

There was no denying that Rafe Edwards

stirred some very strong emotions in her and the fact that he clearly thought she was punishing Billy by taking him to Rainbow House was annoying. Hadn't he been prepared to deliver Billy to the police? He'd soon see that she was right.

His expression certainly changed the moment Dave opened the door and welcomed them in. They must have just finished dinner judging by the rich smell of food. Most of the children were in the playroom, watching television, and the sound of laughter could be heard. Maggie was on the floor in front of the fire, dressing a small baby in a sleep suit. She scooped up the infant and got to her feet in a hurry.

'Oh, my goodness. What's happened? Billy? Oh...' She handed the baby to Dave and enveloped Billy in a hug that was not returned. The boy stood as still as a lamppost.

'This is Rafe Edwards,' Penelope told her. 'He's the pyrotechnician I told you about—the one who did the fireworks at the wedding?'

'Oh...' Maggie held out her hand. 'Welcome

to Rainbow House, Rafe,' she said. 'I'm Maggie. This is Dave. And this is Bianca.' She dropped a kiss on the baby's head. Then it was Penelope's turn to be hugged. 'Good grief, darling. You're soaked. Come upstairs with me while I get baby Bi to bed. We'll find you some dry clothes.' She glanced at Rafe. 'I'm not sure there'd be anything in the chest to fit you, but Dave could find you something.'

'I'm fine.' The sullen expression had given way to…nothing. It was as if the Rafe that Penelope knew had simply vanished. This was a man with no opinion. No charisma. No hint of mischief.

'Stand over by the fire, then, at least. Dave'll get you something hot to drink. Billy? You want to come and find some dry clothes?'

'Nah.' Billy's head didn't move but his glance slid sideways. 'Reckon I'll stand by the fire, too.'

Maggie shared a glance with Penelope, clearly curious about the relationship of the stranger to the boy she knew, but she wasn't going to ask. Not yet. Best let her visitors settle in first. Penelope knew she'd accept them no matter what story had brought them here, and she loved Maggie for the way you became a part of this family simply by walking through the door. When Dave handed her the baby, she was more than happy to take her and cuddle her as she followed Maggie out of the room. Pressing her lips to the downy head was a delicious comfort. It eased the worry of glancing back to see Rafe and Billy both standing like statues in front of the fire.

Rafe had the curious feeling that he'd fallen down one of those rabbit holes in Alice's wonderland.

Had he really thought that Penelope came here occasionally as her contribution to society to read stories to the children or something? She was a part of this family. In this extraordinary house that felt exactly like a *real* home. It even smelt like one. The aroma of something like roast beef made his stomach growl. The heat of the fire was coming through his soaked clothing now, too. A sideways glance showed steam coming off Billy's jeans and the kid had finally stopped shivering. He kind of liked it that Billy had chosen to stay with him, instead of disappearing with the others to find dry clothes. Maybe he felt the connection. Felt like he might have an ally.

Not that Rafe had any qualms about leaving him here, if that was possible. This wasn't like any children's home he'd ever experienced. Hell, it wasn't even like any foster home he'd been dumped in. No point in wondering what kind of difference it might have made if there'd been a place like Rainbow House in his junior orbit. Water under the bridge. A long way under the bridge, and he still didn't want to go swimming in it again. The sooner he got out of here, the better.

Dave had gone to the kitchen and the silence was getting noticeable.

'So you've been here before?'

'Yeah...'

'Not bad, is it?'

'Nah...I guess.'

Dave reappeared with two steaming mugs. 'Soup,' he announced. 'Lucky we always have a pot on the back of the stove.'

Maggie and Penelope appeared by the time he'd taken his first sip and he almost slopped the mug as he did a double-take. What was Penelope wearing?

An ancient pair of trackpants, apparently. And a thick, oversized red woollen jersey that had lumpy white spots all over it. She was still rubbing at her hair with a towel and when she put it down he could see damp ringlets hanging down her back. She had *curly* hair?

She looked so young. Kind of like the way she'd looked in her PJs, only a bit scruffier.

Cute...

The power-dressing princess seemed like a different person. Of course she did. It *was* a different person. Just part of the same, intriguing package that had so many layers of wrapping.

A teenaged girl with improbably blue hair

walked through the living room on her way to the kitchen.

'Hey, Billy. How's it going?' She didn't wait for an answer. 'Dave—John's got the remote and he's not sharing.'

A shriek was heard coming from the playroom. Dave shook his head. 'Excuse me for a moment.'

Maggie clucked her tongue as the blue-haired girl came back. 'Charlene, go back and get a spoon. It's bad manners to eat ice cream with your fingers.'

A snort of something like mirth came from Billy and Penelope caught Rafe's gaze as she came closer to the fire. *This is good*, the glance said. *This is where this kid needs to be.*

She was right. Eventually, there was time to explain why they were here. They were listened to and questions were asked that got right to the heart of the matter.

'You live near the quarry, don't you, Billy? Is that where you go when you need to get away from home?'

Billy shrugged.

'You know it's breaking the law, don't you? The quarry's a dangerous place and that's why there's no public access allowed.'

Another shrug.

'Breaking rules just gets you into trouble, Billy,' Penelope added quietly. 'You *know* that.'

'We'd love to have you back here,' Maggie said, 'And, if you want, Dave'll give Social Services a ring in a minute. Do you think you'd like that to happen?'

The silence was broken by a sniff. Billy scrubbed at his nose, his head still bent so his face couldn't be seen.

'Yeah…I guess.'

'You'd have to follow our rules. Not like last time, okay?'

''Kay.'

'Any knives in your pocket?' Dave's voice was stern.

This time Billy glanced up. Rafe frowned at him.

A pocket knife came out of a back pocket and was handed to Dave.

'Matches?'

The packet of matches that was produced and handed over was too soggy to be a danger but the message was clear. Rules were to be followed and, if they weren't, there would be consequences.

But these were good rules. Rules that kept kids safe. Rafe nodded approvingly.

With a phone call made and permission given to keep Billy at Rainbow House for the time being, the chance to escape finally arrived. Weirdly, Rafe wasn't in a hurry any more. He stayed where he was, as Maggie bundled Penelope's wet clothes into a plastic shopping bag and farewells were made.

Penelope spoke quietly to Billy. 'I'll see you when I'm back on Sunday. Don't tell the others but I'll make a cake that's especially for you. What sort do you like?'

'Chocolate.'

'No problem. And, Billy...?'

'What?'

She was speaking quietly but Rafe could hear every word. 'You don't have to break rules to get people to notice you. It's when you follow the rules that people like you and the more people like you, the more likely you are to get what *you* want.'

What? At least the astonished word didn't get spoken aloud but Rafe had to step away and take a deep breath. Did she really believe that?

Probably. It might explain why this woman was such a complicated mix of contradictory layers. Whose rules was she following? And why did it matter so much that she was liked by whoever was setting those rules? Hadn't she learned by now that what really mattered was whether you liked yourself?

Self-respect. Self-belief.

Obviously not. Man…someone must have done a good job on her self-esteem at some point in her life.

Not his problem. None of what was going on here was his problem and he didn't want to get any more involved. He pulled a phone from his pocket.

'What's the address here?' he asked Dave. 'I'll just call a taxi.'

'No…' Penelope turned away from Billy. 'I can drop you home. It's the least I can do. You saved Billy's *life*…'

A look flashed between Maggie and Dave. A look that suggested she thought there was more going on between him and Penelope than met the eye. Oh, help… Had she heard *all* about the night of the fireworks?

'That's a much better idea,' Maggie said, turning her gaze on Rafe.

He almost grinned. It would be a brave man who went against what this loving but formidable woman thought best.

'Fine.' It came out sounding almost as grudging as Billy had about getting something he was lucky to be offered. He put an apologetic note in his voice. 'I'm a bit out of town, though.'

'No problem.' Penelope stuffed her feet into

her damp shoes and picked up the bag of clothing. 'We've still got some samosas in the back if we get hungry.'

Penelope followed the directions to take the main road out of town and then the turn-off towards the New Forest.

'I've been here before. It's the way to Loxbury Hall.'

'Mmm.'

The only sound for a while then was the rough rumble of the old truck and the swish of the windscreen wipers. The heater still worked well, though, and Penelope was starting to feel too warm in Maggie's old jersey. The T-shirt she had on underneath wasn't enough to stop the itch of the thick wool. She couldn't wait to get home and put her own clothes on. Fire up her straighteners and sort out her hair, too.

Good grief…she must look an absolute fright. This was worse than being caught wearing her pyjamas. At least her hair had been smooth and under control.

'What was that for?'

'What?'

'That groan. I did tell you I was out of town a bit.'

Penelope cringed inwardly. And then sighed aloud. 'It's not that. I'm just a bit over you seeing me at my worst, that's all. A girl thing.'

There was another silence and then Rafe spoke quietly.

'Maybe I'm seeing you at your best.'

She tried to figure that out. Couldn't. 'What's that supposed to mean?'

'You do realise you broke the rules, don't you?'

'What rules?'

'The safety regulations that are a legal obligation for anyone who runs a business like mine. I should be filing a "Near Miss" incident report. Billy should have been charged with trespass.'

'And you think that would have helped him?

For God's sake, Rafe. He's a kid whose home life stinks.'

'And you stood up for him. You were prepared to break the rules to stand up for him. I'm impressed.'

Impressed? With *her*?

Should she feel this pleased that she'd impressed a pyrotechnician cowboy her grandparents would probably consider riff-raff?

Moot point. The pleasure was irresistible and felt inexplicably genuine. And then he went and spoiled it.

'What were you thinking, telling him that people only like you if you follow all the rules?'

'It's true.'

But she could hear the note of doubt in her voice and this man, sitting beside her, was responsible for that. Rafe didn't automatically follow anybody's rules but he had the kind of charisma that no doubt had women falling at his feet with a single glance. He'd won over a small, troubled boy who had probably never trusted anyone in his short life so far. And even Maggie had fallen for him, judging by the way she'd acted when she'd taken Penelope away to find those dry clothes.

Instead of opening the old chest, she'd sat on the top and fanned her face with her hand, giving her a glance that had made Penelope feel she was in the company of young Charlene instead of the warm-hearted and practical woman who was in charge of Rainbow House.

'I'm not a bit surprised you went upstairs at Loxbury Hall with *him*. I'd have been more than a bit tempted myself.'

'Like' was far too insipid a word to describe how Penelope felt about Rafe but she wasn't going to try and analyse those strong emotions. They were dangerous. The kind of emotions that led to trouble. Shame. Sometimes, even death…

Rafe's voice brought the wild train of her thoughts to a crashing halt.

'Did you follow all the rules today? Do you think I like you less because you didn't?'

She didn't respond. There was a note in his voice that suggested he didn't like her much anyway.

'Turn in here.'

'Are you kidding?' But Penelope slowed as the iron gates of Loxbury Hall came up on the left.

Rafe pulled out his phone, punched in a few numbers and the gates began to swing open.

She jammed on the brakes and they came to a grinding halt.

It was quite hard to get the words out. 'When you said you'd cleared it with the owner about going upstairs, you hadn't actually talked to anyone, had you?'

'Nope.'

'Because you *are* the owner?'

'Yep.'

Oh, no... Penelope let her head drop onto the steering-wheel on top of her hands. Now she felt like a complete idiot. Someone who'd been played like a violin.

'Um...Penny?'

She didn't bother to correct the use of the loathed diminutive. 'Yeah…?'

'Do you think you could get us off the road properly before someone comes along and rear-ends us? Just to the front steps would be grand.'

The front steps belonged to the property he'd acquired by not following all the rules. He'd got to where he was in life because he'd believed in himself, not because he'd made other people like him.

Billy could do with a message like that.

Not that he wanted to go anywhere near Rainbow House again. It was sorted. This was it. Time to say goodbye to Ms Penelope Collins.

He turned towards her to do exactly that but then he hesitated. Rain beat a steady rhythm on the roof of the truck and it got suddenly heavier. A flash of lightning made Penelope jump and her eyes got even wider at the enormous crack of thunder that came almost instantly.

'The storm's right on top of us. You can't drive

in this.' Without thinking, Rafe leaned over and pushed back a stray curl that was stuck to Penelope's cheek. 'Come inside till it blows over.'

She wasn't looking at him. And she shook her head.

He should have left it there but he couldn't. He knew an upset woman when he saw one. Had it been something he'd said? His hand was still close to her face and his fingers slipped under her chin to turn her head towards him. At the same time he was racking his brains to think of what it was that had sent her back into her shell. Revealing that he owned Loxbury Hall? No. That had nothing to do with her. Ah… As soon as Penelope's gaze met his, he knew exactly what it was.

'I still like you,' he murmured. 'Breaking the rules only made me like you more.'

Her lips parted and the tip of her tongue appeared and then touched her top lip—as though she wanted to say something but had no idea how to respond. The gesture did something very strange to Rafe's gut. The look in her eyes did something to his heart.

She looked lost. *Afraid*, even?

He had to kiss her. Gently. Reassuringly. To communicate something that seemed very important. And, just in case the kiss hadn't got the message across, he spoke quietly, his lips still moving against hers.

'You're beautiful, Penny. Always believe that.'

A complete stillness fell for a heartbeat. There was nothing but the butterfly-wing softness of that contact lingering between their lips. A feeling of connection like nothing Rafe had ever felt in his life.

And then there was a blinding flash of light. A crack of thunder so loud it felt like the van was rocking. Penelope's body jerked and she emitted a stifled shriek.

That did it. Rafe moved without thinking, out of his seat and running to the driver's side of the van. He wrenched open the door and helped Penelope out. He held her against his body and tried to shelter her inside his jacket but even in the short time it took to get across the driveway and up the steps to the front door of his house was enough for them both to be soaked all over again.

Thank goodness for the efficient central heating in this part of the vast old house. But it wasn't enough. Penelope was shivering.

'I could get a fire started.' He was feeling frozen himself.

'Th-that would be n-nice…'

Was the fire already set or would he have to go hunting for kindling and wood?

'It could take a while.' Which wasn't good enough. And then inspiration struck. 'How 'bout a hot bath?'

'Oh…' She looked for all the world as if he'd captured the moon and was offering it to her in his hands. 'I haven't had a bath in…in for ever. I've only g-got a shower at my p-place.'

Rafe felt ten feet tall. With a decisive nod, he walked towards the staircase. 'You'll love my bath,' he said. 'It's well big enough for two people.'

At the foot of the stairs, he had to stop. Why wasn't she following him? Turning his head, he smiled encouragingly and held out his hand.

'You're quite safe. I wasn't actually suggesting that I'm intending to *share* your bath. I just meant that it would be big enough.'

When she took his hand, hers felt like a small block of ice. Weird that it made him feel so warm inside.

As if he was the one who was being given the moon?

CHAPTER SEVEN

HAVING RAFE IN a bathtub with her was crazy.

It also seemed to be the most natural thing in the world.

How had it happened? Penelope had been sitting there, on the closed lid of the toilet, with a big, fluffy towel around her like a shawl while Rafe supervised the filling of the enormous tub. The tap was one of those old-fashioned, wide, single types and the water rushed out with astonishing speed, filling the room with steam. Steam that became very fragrant when Rafe upended a jar of bath salts into the flow. Then he found a bottle of bubble bath and tipped that in as well.

'You may as well use them up,' he said. 'I'm not likely to.'

So the steam smelled gorgeous and the room

was warm but Penelope could see that Rafe was shivering.

'You need that bath as much as I do. More… You've been in wet clothes for hours.'

'I'll go and have a shower in another bathroom.' But Rafe had turned his head on his way out and met her gaze and it felt like time had suddenly gone into slow motion. 'Unless…?'

And so here they were. Sitting at either end of this wonderful old, claw-footed bathtub, with Rafe slightly lopsided to avoid the tap and Penelope's legs between his. The bubbles covered her chest enough to be perfectly decent and she kept her knees slightly bent so that her toes didn't touch anything they shouldn't.

For the longest time they simply sat there in silence, soaking up the delicious warmth.

'I've never done this before,' she finally confessed. 'As soon as I got old enough, I wouldn't even let my nanny stay in the bathroom with me.'

'You had a *nanny*?'

Penelope swept some bubbles together with her

hands and shaped them into a hill. 'Only because my grandmother didn't want to be a mother
again. She'd done it once, she said, and that was
enough.'

'I hope it was a nice nanny.'

'She was okay. Rita—our housekeeper—was
better. She's the one who taught me to cook and
bake, and by the time I was about eight I was
spending so much time in the kitchen Mother
decided that the nanny was superfluous so they
fired her.'

'A housekeeper and a nanny. Your folks must
be pretty well off.'

'We only had one main bathroom and my grandparents' room had an en suite that had a shower.'
Penelope didn't want to talk about her family any
more. Another scoop of bubbles made the hill
higher. It wobbled but still provided a kind of
wall and it meant she didn't have to look at Rafe
directly. 'How many bathrooms have you got?'

'Haven't really counted.' He sounded vaguely
discomforted by the query. 'A few, I guess.'

Penelope laughed. 'I'd say so.' Her laughter seemed to diffuse the awkwardness. 'What made you want to live here?'

Rafe tipped his head back to rest on the curved rim of the bath. 'I came here once when I was a kid. To a Christmas party. I thought it was the kind of house that only people with a perfect life could ever live in.'

'Were your parents friends of the owners?'

It was Rafe's turn to laugh. 'Are you kidding? I was one of a busload of what they called "disadvantaged" kids. The ones that went to foster homes because they wanted the extra money but then they'd get found out and the kid would get "rescued" so that somewhere better could be found. Somewhere they wouldn't get so abused.'

Shocked, Penelope slid a little further into the water. Her mind was back under that tree, as Clarissa and Blake's vows had been pledged. Seeing that sadness in Rafe's eyes as he'd told her she was one of the lucky ones.

'You know what it's like to have a family. Par-

ents. You know what it's like to live in that safe place...'

Had he thought that a mansion was that kind of safe place when he'd been a little boy? That it would automatically give him a family and mean he was loved?

Penelope wanted to cry. She wanted to reach back through time and take that little boy into her arms and give him the kind of hug that Maggie would give. She wanted to scoop him up and take him to Rainbow House—the way they'd taken Billy today.

That explained the hero-worship, didn't it? Had Billy sensed the connection? Somehow realised he was looking at a role model that he could never have guessed could understand what his life was like?

Maybe her thoughts were hanging in a bubble over her head.

'There weren't any places like Rainbow House back in my day,' Rafe said quietly. 'I wish there had been.' Something like a chuckle escaped.

'Maybe then I wouldn't have broken so many rules.'

Penelope's smile felt wobbly. 'Something went right along the way. Look at where you are now. *Who* you are…'

Her foot moved a little and touched Rafe's leg. His hands must have been under the water, hidden by the layer of foam, because his fingers cupped her calf.

'I'm wondering who *you* are,' he said softly. 'Every time I think I have it figured out, you go and do something else that surprises the heck out of me.'

'Like what?'

'Like breaking the rules. Not shopping Billy in to the cops. Going upstairs with me when you thought it wasn't allowed.'

Oh…help. His fingers were moving on her calf. A gentle massage that was sending tendrils of sensation higher up her leg. More were being generated deep in her belly and they were meeting in the middle in a knot that was both painful and delicious.

'Is not dancing in public one of your rules, too?'

'What?' The exclamation was startled.

'I saw you that day. Dancing in the maze. I was up on the balcony.'

Penelope gasped as something clicked into place. 'How did you know what song I was listening to?'

'You left your iPod on the table in the hall. It wasn't rocket science to check what was played most recently.'

'You were *spying* on me.' Penelope pulled her leg away from his touch. She gripped the side of the bath, stood up and climbed out.

Rafe must have climbed out just as fast because he was right there as she wrapped herself in a towel and turned around. Water streamed off his naked body, taking tiny clumps of bubbles with it. He caught her arms.

'Not *spying*,' he said fiercely. 'I was…intrigued.'

The nearness of him was overwhelming. Nearness and nakedness. She could feel the heat coming off his skin. Smell something masculine that cut through the perfume of the bath salts and bubble bath. His hair hung in damp tendrils and his jaw was shadowed by stubble. And the look in his eyes was...

'I still am,' he murmured. 'You intrigue me, Penelope Collins. No...when you get beneath the layers, I think it would be fairer to say you *amaze* me.'

Penelope forgot how to breathe.

She *amazed* him? On a scale of approving of somebody that was too high to be recognisable. Penelope had never amazed anybody in her life. The highest accolade had been her grandad being proud of her. A nod and even a smile from her grandmother.

Rafe had the world at his feet. He ran a huge, successful company. He'd just bought a house that very few people could ever dream of owning. What did he see in her that could possibly amaze him? It was true, though. She could see the truth of it in the way he was looking at her.

Was it possible for bones to actually *melt* for a heartbeat or two? She was still managing to stand but her fingers were losing their grip on the edges of the towel she had clutched in a bunch between her breasts.

Rafe was still dripping wet. His fingers felt damp enough to leave a cool trail as he reached out and traced the outline of her face but coolness turned into enough heat to feel like her skin was being scorched. Across her temple and cheekbone, down the side of her nose and then over her lips, and still they hadn't looked away from each other's eyes. She could feel the dip to trace the bow of her top lip and then his finger seemed to catch on the cushion of her lower lip.

She saw desire ignite in Rafe's eyes and his face came closer. She could feel his breath on her skin. Could feel his mouth hovering over hers— no more than a hair's breadth from touching— but it couldn't be called kissing.

This was something much deeper than kissing. Something that felt spiritual rather than physical. The waiting was agony but it was also the most wonderful thing Penelope had ever felt. The closeness. The knowing what was coming. The feeling of...*safety*? How amazing was that, that she could feel safe when she was so close to something that she knew could explode with all the ferocity and beauty of one of Rafe's fireworks.

The towel slipped from her fingers as his lips finally made contact. This wasn't just one kiss. It was a thousand kisses. Tiny brushes. Fierce bursts of pressure.

He caught her shoulders as her knees threatened to give up the struggle of keeping her upright. He lifted her. Carried her to where they needed to be.

In his bed.

Rafe didn't turn the bedside light off after he'd ripped the duvet back and placed Penelope in his bed. He wanted to see the look in her eyes as he made love to her. To see if he could catch an expression as extraordinary as the way she'd looked when he'd told her that she amazed him.

And he wanted this to be slow. To last as long as he could make it last because—incredibly—it felt like last time, only better. Still as new and exciting as if it had been the first time ever but familiar, too.

Safe...

She smelled like heaven. She *tasted* like heaven and it had nothing to do with all the stuff he'd tipped into that bath.

It was sex but not as he'd ever known it. This was a conversation that went past anything physical. It felt like simply a need to be together.

And even when the passion was spent, it didn't have to end, did it? He could hold her for a while longer. As long as she was willing to stay?

'Oh, Penny...' Rafe drew her more closely to his body, loving the way her head tucked in against his shoulder. 'Sorry.' His words were a murmur that got buried in her hair. 'Penelope. I forgot how much you hate that.'

'I don't hate it when you say it.' The husky note in her voice was full of the lingering contentment of supreme satiety.

'It's more you.' Rafe could feel his lips curl into a smile and it felt odd—as if he'd never smiled quite like that before. 'It's how I'm going to think of you from now on.'

'How do you mean?'

'It's like "Penelope" has extra layers of letters that hide the real stuff. And it sounds kind of…I don't know…stilted? All professional and polished, anyway. Like you were when you came into my office that day. And how you looked in that silver dress at the wedding.' His breath came out in a soft snort. 'Who knew I'd end up seeing you wearing your PJs? And trackpants and a jersey with big fluffy spots on it?'

'Don't remind me.'

He could feel the way her body tensed. He

pressed his lips against her hair and willed her to relax. And it seemed to work. She sounded amused when she spoke again.

'I was so embarrassed when you caught me in my pyjamas. I only do that when I think no one's going to see me.'

'When you're being Penny instead of Penelope.'

He felt her breasts press against his arms as she sighed. 'My best friend at school called me Penny for a while but I made her stop.'

'Why?'

'There were some older kids there who knew more about me than I did. They told me I'd been called Penny because they're not worth anything any more. That nobody wanted me. That my mother had died because even she didn't want me.'

'Kids can be so cruel.' Rafe stroked her hair. 'What did you say?'

'That my name was Penelope and not Penny. And then I told the teacher about them breaking the rules and smoking behind the bike sheds and they got into a whole heap of trouble.'

'Did it make you feel any better?'

'Not really. And then I went home and started asking questions and that got me into a whole heap of trouble. My mother got one of her migraines and had to go to bed for three days and Grandad told me not to talk about it again. It became a new rule.'

'Sounds like you grew up with a lot of rules.'

'Yep.'

'Like what?'

'Oh, the usual ones. Doing what I was told and not talking back, getting good marks in school, not smoking or drinking. Only going out with nice boys that they approved of.'

Rafe snorted again. 'Would they approve of me?'

Penelope sounded like she was smiling but her tone was wry. 'After what we've just been doing? I doubt it very much.'

'Breaking another rule, huh? Lucky me.' He

pressed another kiss to her tangled hair. 'Guess I'm a bad influence.'

'More likely it's my bad blood finally coming out. And you know what?' Penelope turned in his arms before he could answer. 'Right now, I don't even care.' She lifted her face and kissed him.

It was true. How could something that felt this right be so wrong, anyway? She waited, in that moment of stillness, to hear the old litany about her turning out just like her mother but, strangely, it didn't come. Maybe it would hit her on the way home, in which case she might as well stay exactly where she was for a bit longer. Maybe she could just go to sleep here in his arms. How perfect would that feel?

But Rafe didn't sound sleepy.

'Bad *blood*? What the heck is that?'

'Oh, you know. A genetic tendency to do bad stuff. Like take drugs or have wild sex with strangers.'

'I'm pretty sure you don't have "bad" blood.'

He sounded amused now. 'It was probably one of the rules you grew up with. No bad blood allowed.'

'Pretty much. Nurture had to win over nature. Which is why I was never allowed to ask any questions about my father. That's where I got my bad blood from. He was the one who led my mother astray. Got her into drugs. Got her pregnant at sixteen. Made her run away from home so my grandparents never saw her again. Until she was dead.'

'I don't do drugs,' Rafe said quietly. 'And you're not going to get pregnant if I can help it. I do have a few rules of my own. In my case, nature probably won out over nurture.'

'I'm not sixteen. I get to do what I choose now.' It had been true for a very long time but this was the first time it *felt* true. She was choosing to be here and stay here for a bit longer because…because it felt so good.

'But you wouldn't tell your grandmother.'

'No. Only because it would hurt Grandad so

much. He loves her. He loves me, too, but his priority has always been to protect Mother. And I get that. I think their lives got ruined when they lost their daughter. My mother.'

'What was her name?'

She hesitated for a long moment. She never talked about this. She'd never told anyone her mother's name. But this was Rafe and she felt safe. The word still came out as a whisper.

'Charlotte.'

There was a long silence then. Penelope was absorbing how it made things seem more real when you spoke them. How weird it was to have had a mother who'd never existed in reality as far as she was concerned.

Rafe seemed content to leave her in peace. Had he fallen asleep?

No. He must have been thinking about her. About her unusual parentage.

'Have you ever wanted to find out who your father was?'

'I know his name. It was on my birth certificate.'

'What was it?'

'Patrick Murphy. How funny is that?'

'Why funny?'

'They're probably the two most common Irish names there are. Imagine trying to search for him.'

'Have you…imagined, at least?'

'Of course. But maybe it's better not to know anything more.'

'What *do* you know—other than his name?'

'That he played a guitar in a band. Took drugs and got girls pregnant and then left town and never saw them again. Doesn't sound like a very nice person, does he?'

'There are always two sides to every story, darling.'

Darling…nobody had ever called her that before. It sent a weird tingle through Penelope's body. Embarrassingly, it made her want to cry. Or maybe there was more to the prickle behind her eyes than the endearment.

'He didn't want me,' she whispered. 'Any more

than my mother did. She *left* me…under a bush. Who does that to their baby?'

'Maybe she had no choice.' Could he hear the imminent tears in her voice? Was that why he was holding her so close? Pressing his cheek against her head as if he could feel her pain? And more…as if he wanted to make it go away.

Nobody could do that. It was ancient history.

'There's something I should tell you. It happened a few weeks ago. The night after we… the night after the wedding here.' The pressure on her head was easing—as if Rafe was creating some distance because he was about to tell her something uncomfortable. 'I went to a party with some old mates. A band I used to be part of. There was a girl there…'

Oh, *no*… Was he about to tell her he was in a relationship with someone? That this was nothing more than a bit on the side? Penelope braced herself for something huge. Something that had the potential to hurt her far more than she had a right to let it.

'She was a journalist. Julie, I think her name was.'

Penelope didn't need to know this. Her muscles were bunching. Getting ready to propel her out of Rafe's bed.

Out of his life.

'Anyway, she's interested in a story. About a baby they called Baby X.'

Penelope went very, very still. There was relief there that he didn't seem to be telling her about a woman who was important in his life but there was fear, too. This was something that was supposed to be hidden. Long forgotten.

'Apparently Baby X was found under a bush. At the Loxbury music festival, nearly thirty years ago.'

There were tears running down Penelope's cheeks. 'That was me,' she whispered. 'It's going to be my thirtieth birthday in a couple of weeks.'

'I'm guessing you wouldn't want someone turning up on your doorstep, asking questions?'

'*No...*' Penelope squeezed her eyes shut. 'Or, even worse, chasing my folks. They'd *hate* that.' She swallowed hard. 'You don't think they'll be able to find out, do you?'

'I don't know. I'm surprised it's been kept such a secret for so long. It's the kind of story people love to know there's a happy ending to.'

'Grandad was pretty high up in the police force back then. He might have pulled a few strings to have things kept quiet. People knew that my mother had died, of course, and that I was an orphan. But I'm pretty sure no one got told *how* she died or where she was at the time.'

'So there's no way to connect her to Baby X, then. You should be safe.'

But there was a note of doubt in Rafe's voice and Penelope felt it, too. Why hadn't anyone made what seemed like an obvious connection?

More disturbingly, what would happen if they did?

'I should go,' she said. 'Maybe I should have a word with Grandad and warn him.'

'Don't go. Not yet.' Rafe's arms tightened around her. 'It's still raining out there. Why not wait till the morning?'

How good would it be to push that all aside and not worry about it yet? If she stayed here and slept in Rafe's arms, would he make love to her again in the morning?

'Julie's actually coming to see me at the office tomorrow. I've offered to do a fireworks show at the close of the festival as a contribution to the charity they're supporting. I could find out how much she knows already. Whether there's a chance they'll find out who you are. I could try and put her off even, if you'd like. Warn her that she could do some damage to people if she pursued a story that would be better left alone.'

He'd do that? For her?

'Thank you. I'd owe you a big favour if you could do that.'

'You wouldn't owe me anything.' Rafe was

smiling. 'I told you, Penny. I like you. I like you a lot.'

'I like you, too.'

She gave herself up to his kiss then, and it was easy to put any other thoughts aside. So easy to sink into the bliss of touching and being touched.

Except that one thought wasn't so easy to dismiss. Again, 'like' was too insipid a word to have used when it came to Rafe.

She felt protected. Chosen. Loved—even if that was only a fantasy on her part.

It was no fantasy in the other direction. God help her, but she was in love with Rafe Edwards. She probably had been ever since he'd chosen the song she'd been dancing to for his fireworks show. Knowing that he had done so after seeing her dancing had shocked her, but now it made it all seem inevitable. How could you not fall in love with a man who'd chosen a song he knew would make you dance?

A man who was amazed by you?

The potential fallout of having her past and

her family's shame made public was huge. And frightening.

But it wasn't nearly as big as how she felt about Rafe, so she could still feel safe while she was here. She could catch this moment of a happiness she'd never known existed.

Tomorrow would just have to take care of itself.

CHAPTER EIGHT

PENNY WAS GONE from his bed long before dawn broke. It was a downside of working in the food industry, apparently. If they had a large gig to cater, the kitchens opened for work by four a.m. She didn't go in this early very often now, because her role was changing to event management, but she'd told Jack she wanted to be in charge of this particular event.

It was a special occasion, apparently. Something to do with the Loxbury City Council and her grandfather would be there so she wanted everybody to be impressed.

'And I have to go home first. Can you imagine what people would think if I turned up in track pants and a spotty jersey, with my hair looking like *this*?'

She actually giggled and it was the most delicious sound he'd ever heard. No...that prize had to go to that whimper of pure bliss he'd drawn from her lips not so long ago.

But, yeah...he could imagine. They'd be blown away by seeing a side of their boss they'd never seen before. A glimpse of Penny instead of Penelope.

But she never let people see that side, did she?

Maybe he was the only person who'd ever got this close to her?

That made him feel nervous enough to chase away the possibility of getting back to sleep.

And his bed felt oddly empty after she'd gone anyway, so he shoved back the covers and headed for the shower.

The bath was still full of water from last night. The bubbles had gone, leaving only patches of scum floating on the surface of a faintly green pond. With a grimace, Rafe plunged his arm into the icy-cold water and pulled the plug.

Just like he'd have to pull the plug on whatever was happening between himself and Penny at some point down the track? His nervousness morphed into something less pleasant. He avoided looking in the mirror as he moved to the toilet because he had a feeling he wouldn't like the person he'd see.

Somebody who'd let someone get close and then leave town and never see her again?

The puddle of the towel on the tiled floor was in the way of getting to the shower cubicle. Rafe stooped and picked it up, remembering the way it had slipped from Penny's body as he'd been kissing her last night. He could almost swear a faint scent of her got released from the fabric as he dropped it into the laundry basket. He heard himself groan as he reached into the shower and flicked on the taps.

It wasn't that he was setting out to hurt her. He just didn't do anything long-term. What was the point of making promises that only ended up getting broken? That was when people got really hurt.

She was too vulnerable for him. And her belief that marriage was some sacred promise that made everything perfect was downright scary. She would probably deny it—he'd seen that magazine article where she'd said she was a happily single career-woman—but the truth was she was searching for 'the one.' The man who'd marry her and give her a bunch of babies.

And that man wasn't him.

No way.

Funny how empty his house felt when she'd gone. How empty *he* felt.

Well, that was a no-brainer. How had they completely forgotten to have any dinner last night? A fry-up would fix that. Bacon and eggs and some mushrooms, along with some thick slices of toast and a good slathering of butter.

By the time he'd finished that, he might as well go into work himself. He'd promised a show to remember for the anniversary Loxbury music festival and the pressure was on to get it planned and organised.

It was a weird twist of fate that the original festival had such significance in Penny's life but a seed of something that felt good came in thinking about that connection. He might not be able to give her what she wanted in life but he could do something to protect her right now. To stop other people hurting her.

Yes. By the time Rafe locked the door of his vast, empty house behind him and walked out into the new dawn, he was feeling much better.

He could fix something. Or at least make sure it didn't get any more broken than it already was.

Julie the journalist was young—probably in her early twenties—and she had an enthusiasm that made Rafe feel old and wise in comparison.

She was also cute, trying to look professional in her summery dress and ballet flats, with her hair up in a messy kind of bun.

Compared to Penny in professional mode, she looked like a child playing dress-up. She was a bit of a chatterbox, too, and giggled often enough for it to become annoying. Was she flirting with him?

If so, she had no idea how far off the mark she was. He couldn't be less interested but he kept smiling. He might need her cooperation on something important if the opportunity arose to put her off chasing the Baby X story. No, make that when. He'd make sure that opportunity arose.

There was plenty to show her and talk about before that. Video clips of old shows, for instance.

'This was the Fourth of July in Times Square. A bigger show than the one we're planning for the festival but we'll be using a lot of the same kind of fireworks. And this is a much more recent one.'

'Oh…isn't that the Summers wedding? I've seen that already. Love the hearts. And it's a cool song…' Julie's head was swaying and her hands were moving. He couldn't imagine any inhibitions about dancing in public with this girl. Any moment now she'd probably jump onto his desk and start dancing.

An image of Penny dancing in the maze moved in the back of his mind. Awkward. Endearing…

'That's one of the early challenges, picking the right song for a show. And it's important to get it locked in because that's when the planning really starts. Hitting the right breaks with the right shells. Making it a work of art instead of just a lot of noise and colour.'

'So have you chosen the song for the festival?'

'Mmm. Did that first thing this morning.'

'What is it?'

'I can't tell you that. If word got out, it wouldn't be a surprise and it would lose a lot of its impact.'

'Oh…*please*…?' Julie's eyes were wide as she leaned closer. 'I cross my heart and hope to die promise that I won't tell *anybody*.'

She was desperate to know. And if he gave her what she wanted, would she be more likely to return the favour?

'Okay…but this has to be a secret. Just between us.'

Her nod was solemn. Rafe made his tone just as serious.

'The first festival was held in 1985. The first thing I did was search for all the number-one hits for that year. And then I looked for ones that would work well with fireworks.'

'And…?'

'Strangely enough, Jennifer Rush's "Power of Love" was one of them.' And hadn't that hit him like a brick. How long had he sat there, the list blurring on the screen in front of him, as he re-lived watching Penny watching his fireworks that night. That first kiss…

'But you've already used that recently, yes?'

'Yeah…then I found another one and remembered something big that happened in 1985. In May. Only a few months before the festival so anyone who was there would remember it very well.'

'Bit before my time.' Julie smiled. 'You'll have to enlighten me.'

'The Bradford stadium fire? Killed a bunch of people and injured a whole lot more. It was a real tragedy.'

Julie frowned. 'Doesn't sound like a good connection to remind people of.'

'That's the thing. A group that called themselves The Crowd released a song to help with the fundraising effort and it's a song that everybody knows. An anthem that's all about exactly that—connection between people and the strength that they can give each other.'

'Wow…so, are you going to tell me what this magic song is?'

'Better than that.' Rafe clicked his mouse. 'Have a listen…'

A few minutes later and Julie was looking misty. 'That's just perfect…' She sniffed. 'I'd love to use it in my story but it'll still make great copy for a follow-up review.'

'There should be lots of great stuff to follow up on. Did you know that they've got a lot of the original artists playing again?'

'And current ones—like Diversion. Are you going to play with them? Matt really wants you to.'

Was there something going on between Diversion's lead singer and Julie? Rafe made a mental note to ask his mate what he thought he was doing when he saw the guys at the pub straight after this. Julie was too young. She'd end up getting hurt.

'I'm thinking about it. It'd be fun but I'll be pretty busy setting up the show.'

Julie folded her notepad and picked up her shoulder-bag. She looked like she was getting ready to leave.

'It can't be just the fireworks you're checking up on for your piece about the festival,' he said casually. 'What else is interesting?'

'Well, there's some debate about what charity is going to benefit from the profits. Last time it was the Last Wish Foundation for terminally sick kids and the time before that it was cancer research, but they want something local this time. It's all about Loxbury.'

'Mmm.' Rafe tried to sound interested instead of impatient. 'What about that other story? The girl who died?'

'Oh…' Julie's face lit up and she let her bag slip off her shoulder to land on the floor again. 'Now, that's *really* interesting. I had to call in a few favours to get any information but I finally tracked it down through someone who had access to old admission data at Loxbury General's A and E department. There were a few girls to choose from that day but only one who was really sick.'

'From a drug overdose?'

'That's the interesting bit. It was a bit of a scandal at the time because everyone assumed it *was* a drug overdose.'

'And it wasn't?'

'No. Apparently there was no trace of drugs. The coroner listed the death as being from natural causes. The poor girl had a brain aneurysm. She got taken off life support a few days after she'd collapsed at the festival.'

Why didn't Penny know that? Why had she been allowed to think that her mother had been some kind of drug addict who'd abandoned her in favour of finding a high? He'd suggested that maybe she'd had no choice other than to leave her baby under a bush. Having a brain haemorrhage certainly came under that category, didn't it? Wouldn't it have caused a dreadful headache or something? Scrambled thoughts enough for the sufferer to not be thinking straight?

'I got lucky.' Julie tapped the side of her nose. 'I got her name. Charlotte Collins. I've been trying to contact her family but do you know how many Collinses there are in Loxbury?'

She didn't wait for him to guess, which was just as well because Rafe was still thinking about Penny. How it might change things if she knew the truth. But, then, why hadn't she already been told? What kind of can of worms might he be opening?

'A hundred and thirty-seven,' Julie continued. 'And this Charlotte might not even have been local.' She paused for a breath. 'Mind you, I did get an odd reaction of this dead silence with one call. And then the phone got slammed down.

The number was for a Douglas Collins. He got an OBE for service to the police force and now he's got some important job in the city council. I might follow that up again.'

'Don't you think it would be kind of intrusive to have someone asking about the death of your child?'

'But it was thirty years ago.' Julie looked genuinely surprised. 'I'd think they might like to think that someone remembered her. I might suggest some kind of tribute at the festival even, if I can find out a bit more.'

'I wouldn't.' Rafe summoned all the charm he could muster. 'I'd let the poor girl just rest in peace.'

'Oh…' Julie was holding his gaze. 'Really? But doesn't it strike you as too much of a coincidence that a girl died *and* there was an abandoned baby found? There's got to be a connection, don't you think?'

'Is that why you're chasing the story of the dead girl?'

'It's the only lead I've got. I can't find anything out about the baby. All I've got to go on is that they thought it was a few days old and there was a mention in the news that it had been reunited with family a short time later. Nobody ever said *why* it got left under a bush, though.'

'I guess the family wanted privacy. Maybe that should be respected.'

Julie didn't seem to hear him. 'Do you know how many babies get born in Britain?' She had a habit of asking questions she intended to answer herself. 'One every forty seconds or so. That's a lot of babies. Even if you have an approximate birth date you've got hundreds and hundreds to choose from, but guess what?'

'What?'

'Last night, I found one with the surname of Collins. Born in London but guess what the mother's name on the birth record is?'

Rafe didn't want to guess. He already knew.

'Charlotte,' Julie whispered. 'But that's just between us, okay? I'll keep your secret about the song and you can keep mine.'

'So you're looking for this daughter now?'

'You bet. But I've got a long way to go. What if she got adopted and has a completely different name now?'

'What if she's adopted and doesn't know about it? You could damage a whole family.'

'She's all grown up now. I'm sure she could cope. She might even like her five minutes of fame.'

Rafe stood up. He couldn't say anything else but he needed to move. He wasn't doing a very good job of putting Julie off the scent, was he? How could he protect Penny?

He really, really wanted to protect her.

Somehow.

'As you said, it's a common name. I suspect you'll find a dead end.'

'No such thing in journalism.' Julie beamed at him. 'It just means there's a new direction to try. And I've got one to go and try right now. Thanks for the interview, Rafe. I'll look forward to seeing the fireworks.'

* * *

There might be fireworks of an entirely different kind well before the festival, Rafe mused, leaving his office to get to the pub where his old mates were waiting to have a beer and talk about whether he was going to join the band for a song or two on the day.

As soon as he'd had a beer or two he'd get away. At least he and Penny had exchanged phone numbers now. He could call her and warn her about how close Julie was getting to the truth. Apologise for not being more effective in throwing her off the scent, but how could he when she was so far down the track already? He could do it now, in fact, before he went somewhere noisy. Stopping in the street, he pulled his phone from his pocket. He dialled her number but, as it began to ring, another thought struck him.

Maybe he should also tell her that the truth was not what she believed it to be. But that wasn't something he could tell her over the phone. Cutting the call off, he shoved his mobile back into his pocket. It was a good thing he knew where she lived. A smile tugged at his lips as he pushed his way into a crowded Irish bar. Maybe there was a chance she'd be wearing those PJs again when she opened her door. If he stayed a bit longer at the pub with his mates, the odds of that being the case would only get stronger.

There was a good band playing and the beer was even better. Telling Scruff and Matt and the others that he'd like to get up on stage with them for old times' sake led to a lot of back-slapping and a new round of beer, this time with some whisky shots as well.

'You'll love it, man. Can't wait to tell the Twickenham twins. Bet they'll turn up with their pompoms as well as their cowboy hats. Hey, let's give them a call. They might like a night out, too.'

'I can't stay too long. Somewhere to be soon.'

'You can't leave yet. Band's not bad, eh? For a bunch of oldies.'

Rafe took another glance at the group on stage.

'They're no spring chickens, are they? Best place for Irish music, though. They wouldn't sound half as good at an outdoor gig.'

'Don't let them hear you say that. They'll be playing at the festival. They're one of the original acts that's being brought back.'

Rafe peered at the set of drums. 'What's with the name? The *Paws*?'

'Bit of a laugh, eh? I hear it got picked because it's the nickname of the lead guitarist but it got a lot funnier after the Corrs came along.'

'What kind of a nickname is Paws?' Rafe had another look as a new round of drinks got delivered to their corner. 'His hands look perfectly normal to me.'

'That's not normal. Listen to him—the guy's a genius. Paddy's his real name. Good name for an Irish dude, eh?'

'Don't tell me,' Rafe grinned. 'His surname's Murphy?'

Scruff's jaw dropped. 'You knew all along, didn't you?'

'No.' This time Rafe couldn't take his eyes off the guitarist. Paws. Paddy. Patrick. A Patrick Murphy who played the guitar. Who'd been at the Loxbury music festival thirty years ago? What were the odds?

Maybe Julie was right. Dead ends only led to a new direction. If the truth was going to come out, maybe the best thing he could do for Penny was to make sure that the *whole* truth came out. And this was too much of a coincidence to ignore.

Maybe he'd wait until the band finished for the night. Buy the guy a beer and at least find out if he'd ever known a girl called Charlotte Collins. Get a feel for whether there was any point in going any further.

In the meantime, there were drinks to be had. Conversations to be had along with them.

'Hey, Scruff? What did you do with that old set of drums I gave you way back? The ones I got given before I took up the sax?'

'They're still in the back of my garage. Bit of history, they are.'

'D'you really want to keep them?'

'Hadn't thought about it. Guess I should clean out the garage some time so I can fit my car back into it? Why?'

'Just that I met a kid the other day who looks like he could use a direction in life. A set of drums is a good way to burn up a bit of teenage angst, if nothing else.'

'True. Come and get them any time, man. They were yours in the first place, anyway.'

It was the buzzing in his pocket that finally distracted him from what was turning out to be a very enjoyable evening. He would never have heard his phone ringing but he could feel the vibration. When he saw that Penny was the caller, he pushed his way out of the bar again. Out into the relative peace of an inner-city street at night.

'Penny…hey, babe.'

'How *could* you, Rafe? When you knew how important it was…'

Good grief…was she *crying*?

'I trusted you…and then you go and do *this*…'

Yep. She was crying. Either that or she was so angry it was making her words wobble and her voice so tight he wouldn't have recognised it.

'What are you talking about? What am I supposed to have done?'

'Julie.' The word was an accusation. 'You *told* her.'

'Told her what?' But there was a chill running down his spine. He had a bad feeling about this.'

'About me. About my grandparents. She turned up on their doorstep, asking all sorts of questions… Oh, my God, Rafe… Have you any idea what you've *done*?'

'I didn't tell her anything. She'd already figured it out. I was going to tell you…'

'You really expect me to believe that? You told her and then she turned up and now…and now Grandad's probably going to die…'

'What?'

'They got rid of her but Mother was really upset. Rita called me. By the time I got there, all I could do was call an ambulance.' There was the sound of a broken sob on the other end of the line. 'He's had a heart attack and he's in Intensive Care and they don't know if he's even going to make it and…and this is…this is all… Oh, *God*… Why am I even talking to you about this?'

The call ended abruptly. What had she left unsaid? That it was all his fault?

It wasn't true. It wasn't even fair.

But standing there, in the street, with the echoes of that heartbroken voice louder than the beeping of the terminated call, it felt remarkably like it was, somehow, *his* fault.

CHAPTER NINE

THEY WERE TAKING him away.

Penelope watched the bed being wheeled towards the elevator, flanked by a medical team wearing theatre scrubs, the suddenly frail figure of her beloved grandfather almost hidden by the machines that were keeping him alive.

The elevator doors closed behind the entourage and Penelope pressed her hand against her mouth. Was this going to be the last time she saw him alive? He was the only person in her life she could believe still loved her, even when she messed up and broke a rule. Someone who could see some value in what Rafe called Penny instead of Penelope.

Oh, God…she didn't want to think about Rafe right now. About that shock of betrayal that had felt like a death and only made it so much worse as she'd watched the paramedics fighting to stabilise Grandad before rushing him to hospital.

A sideways glance showed her own fear reflected on her grandmother's face but the instinct to move closer and offer the comfort of a physical touch had to be suppressed.

'I'll take you to our family waiting room.' The nurse beside them was sympathetic. 'Someone will come and find you as soon as we know anything.'

'How long is this procedure going to take?' Louise spoke precisely and it sounded as though she was asking about something as unimportant as having her teeth whitened but Penelope knew it was a front. She'd never seen her grandmother looking so pale and frightened.

Lost, even…

'That depends,' the nurse said. 'If the angioplasty's not successful, they'll take Mr Collins straight into Theatre for a bypass operation. We should know whether that's likely within the next hour or so. Here we are…' She opened the door to a small room that contained couches and chairs, a television and a coffee table with a stack of magazines. 'Help yourself to coffee or tea. Milk's in the fridge. If you get hungry, there's a cafeteria on the ground floor that stays open all night.'

The thought of food was nauseating.

The silence, when the nurse had closed the door behind her, was deafening.

Louise sat stiffly on the edge of one of the chairs, staring at the magazines. Was she going to pick one up and make the lack of conversation more acceptable?

'Can I make you a cup of tea, Mother?'

'No, thank you, Penelope.'

'Coffee?'

'No.'

'A glass of water?'

'*No*… For heaven's sake, just leave me alone.' Her voice rose and shook and then—to Penelope's horror—her grandmother's shoulders began shaking. She was *crying*?

'I'm sorry,' she heard herself whisper.

What was she apologising for? Telling Rafe her story, which had been passed on to that journalist who'd been the catalyst for this disaster? How *could* he have done that? She'd felt so safe with him. Had trusted him completely. The anger that had fuelled that phone call had evaporated now, though, leaving her feeling simply heartbroken.

Or was she apologising for being the person her grandmother had to share this vigil with? For all the years that her grandparents had had to share their lives with her when they could have been enjoying their retirement together? Was she apologising for having been born at all?

Or was she just sorry this was happening? Sorry for herself and for Mother and most of all for Grandad.

Maybe it was all of those things.

'He's in the right place,' she said softly. 'And he's a fighter. He won't give up.'

Louise pulled tissues from the box beside the magazines. 'You have no idea what you're talking about, Penelope. This is precisely what *could* make him give up. Being reminded…'

Of what? Losing their daughter and getting the booby prize of a grandchild they hadn't wanted? Penelope didn't know what to say.

Louise blew her nose but kept the tissue pressed against her face so her voice sounded muffled. 'He gave up then. He was in the running for the kind of job that would have earned him a knighthood eventually. A seat in parliament, even, where he could have achieved his life's dream of law reform that would have made a real difference on the front line. There were two things Douglas was passionate about. His job. And his daughter.'

'And you.' Penelope sank onto the couch, facing her grandmother. Louise had never talked to her like this and it was faintly alarming. This was breaking a huge rule—talking about the past. Maybe that was why she was crossing a boundary here, too, in saying something so personal. 'He loves you, too, Mother.'

Louise had her eyes closed as she slumped in her chair. 'I gave him Charlotte,' she whispered. 'That was my biggest accomplishment…but I couldn't stop it happening. I tried *so* hard…'

Penelope's mouth was dry. Was Louise really aware of who she was talking to? It felt like she was listening to someone talking to themselves. Someone whose barriers had crumbled under the weight of fear and impending grief.

'What…?' The word opened a door that was supposed to be locked. 'What was happening?'

'The violin lessons. That was what should have been happening.' The huff of breath was incredulous. 'But, no…we found out she'd given up the lessons. It wasn't hard to have her followed and that's how we found out about the boy.'

Penelope's heart seemed to stop and then deliver a painful thump. 'My…father?'

'Patrick.' The name was a curse. 'A long-haired Irish lout who'd given up his education to be in a band that played in pubs. He was living in a squat, along with his band and their friends—the drug dealers.'

'Oh…' She could understand how distressing that must have been. What if she had a sixteen-year-old daughter who got in with a bad crowd? A reminder of the anger she'd felt towards Rafe surfaced but this time it was directed at the mother she'd never known. A drug addict. Someone who'd made her parents unhappy and then gone on to abandon her own baby. There was something to be said for the mantra she'd been brought up with. Penelope didn't want to end up like her mother. No way.

'She threatened to run away and live with the boy if we tried to stop them seeing each other. They were "in love", she said. They were going to get married and live happily ever after.' For the first time since she'd started talking, she opened her eyes and looked directly at Penelope. 'How ridiculous was that? She barely knew him.'

Penelope had to look away, a confusing jumble of emotions vying for prominence. She barely

knew Rafe but there'd been more than one occasion with him when she'd thought there was
nowhere else in the world she'd ever want to be.
A wave of longing pushed up through the anger.
And then there was that hurt again and somewhere in between there was a flash of sympathy
for her mother. A connection born of understanding the power of that kind of love?

'Douglas was in the final round of interviews
for the new government position. Can you imagine how helpful that would have been? How could
anyone think that he could contribute to law and
order on a national level when he couldn't even
keep his own house in order? When his daughter was living in a drug den?'

Penelope was silent. Maybe it could have been
a point in his favour. Didn't a lot of people become doctors because they hadn't been able to
help a loved one? Have the motivation to help because they understood the suffering that could
be caused? Look at the way Rafe had been with
Billy. He'd known what that boy was going

through and he'd had to step up and help, even when it had clearly been difficult for him. There was something fundamentally good about Rafe Edwards. It was hard to believe he would ever do anything to hurt someone else deliberately. She didn't *want* to believe it but how could she not, when the evidence was right there in front of her?

'It wasn't hard to have the house raided with our police connections. Arrests made.' Louise sounded tired now. 'There wasn't anything that the boy or his band friends could be directly charged with but association was enough. They got warned to get out of town and stay out. *He* was told in no uncertain terms that if he tried to contact Charlotte again, charges could still be laid and they could all find themselves behind bars.'

'So he just left? Even knowing that he was going to be a father?'

Louise fluttered a hand as if it was unimport-ant. 'I don't imagine he knew. I'm not sure Char-

lotte knew. Either that or she kept it hidden until
it was too late to do anything about it.'

Somehow this was the most shocking thing
she'd heard so far in this extraordinary conversation and the words came out in a gasp.

'An abortion, you mean?'

She might not have existed at all and that was
a weird thought. She would never have known
the satisfaction of being successful, doing something she loved. Or felt the pleasures that creating
beautiful food or listening to wonderful music
could provide. She would never have danced. She
would never have experienced the kind of bliss
that Rafe had given her, albeit so briefly.

There was something else she could feel for her
mother now. Gratitude at being protected?

'Of course.' The clipped pronouncement was
harsh. 'Not that your mother would have coop-
erated. She became extremely...difficult. She
stopped eating. Stopped talking. Your grandfather was beside himself. It was the psychiatrist
we took her to who guessed she was pregnant.'

The long silence suggested that the conversation was over as far as Louise was concerned, but Penelope couldn't leave her story there.

'What happened then?'

'I found a boarding school that specialised in dealing with situations like that. She was to stay there and continue her schooling and then the baby would be adopted.'

That baby was *me*. Your grandchild…

But the agonised cry stayed buried. Instead, Penelope swallowed hard and spoke calmly. 'Was Grandad happy about that?'

Louise had her eyes shut again. 'It was a difficult time for all of us but there was no choice. Not if he wanted that promotion.'

A promotion that had clearly never happened.

The silence was even longer this time. Maybe they would hear soon about what was happening with Grandad. No doubt someone would come and talk to them in person but it was an automatic gesture to check her phone. Nothing.

Except a missed call from Rafe.

Hours ago now. Well before she'd called him.

The wash of relief was strong enough to bring the prickle of tears to her eyes. So he had been telling the truth? He had tried to call her? To confess he'd said something he had promised not to and revealed the identity of Baby X?

But why had those questions Julie had been asking had such an effect? Why was it still such a big deal, given that her grandfather had retired so long? This was only getting more confusing.

'How did I end up at the music festival? Do you know?'

Louise shrugged. 'There was a letter that came to the house. From him. Full of ridiculous statements like how he couldn't live without her. That he'd be at the festival and if she felt the same way she could find him there. I didn't forward it, of course, but I presume Charlotte found out somehow. She was in the hospital then, instead of the school, so it was probably wasn't hard to escape.'

Escape… As though she'd been sent to prison.

How hard would it still have been to get away? To take her newborn baby with her?

Penelope felt the ground shifting beneath her feet. She hadn't been abandoned. Her mother could have left her at the hospital but she'd taken her. To the festival. To meet her father?

'We got the call later that day to say she was in the intensive care unit. Right here, in almost the same place as Douglas. How ironic is that? It was obvious she'd recently given birth so we had no choice but to make enquiries about what had happened to the baby. It was your grandfather who insisted on bringing you home. You were the only thing that he cared about after Charlotte died. He gave up on his job and he…he blamed me for sending our daughter away…'

'He still did well. He got an OBE.'

'Hardly a knighthood.'

'He's a well-respected councillor.'

'Not exactly a seat in parliament or a mayoralty, is it? And the passion was never there any more.' Louise was struggling not to cry again. 'I tried to make the best of it. We pulled strings and managed to keep the story out of the papers. I did my best for you but the reminders were always there. And now there's a reporter trying to turn it all into tabloid fodder. Asking questions about why people had been allowed to assume it was a drug overdose when it wasn't. And it's all—'

All what? *Her* fault? Her own fault? What had caused her mother's death if it wasn't a drug overdose? Something that she could have had treated and survived? Had guilt been the poison in her family rather than shame?

The unfinished sentence was an echo of her call to Rafe. And he probably knew that she'd been about to tell him it was all *his* fault. But how could Julie have known it hadn't been a drug overdose? She hadn't told Rafe that because she hadn't known herself.

This was all a huge, horrible mess. And maybe none of it really mattered at the moment, anyway. The door to the room opened quietly to admit the nurse who had brought them here.

'It's all over,' she said. 'And it went very well. Mr Collins is awake now. Would you like to come and see him?'

Louise seemed incapable of getting up from her chair. She had tears streaming down her face. When she looked at Penelope there was an expression she'd never seen before. A plea that could have been for reassurance that she had just heard what she most wanted to hear.

Or could it be—at least partly—a plea for forgiveness?

Penelope held out her hand. 'Let's go,' she said quietly. 'Grandad needs us.'

'So that's about it. The rehearsal starts at five tomorrow. Let's all work together and make this a really family-friendly occasion.'

Rafe glanced at his watch. The meeting of all the key people involved in the organisation and set-up of the Loxbury music festival had filled an impressive section of the town hall. Scruff and Matt were here and he'd noticed Patrick Murphy at the back, no doubt here to find the time his band was expected to turn up for the rehearsal. Surprising how strong the urge still was to seek him out after the meeting and talk to the man who could well be Penelope's father, but he'd already done enough damage as far as she was concerned and he had no desire to get any more involved.

It was over. Or it would be, when he could shake this sense of...what was it? He hadn't done anything wrong in the first place and he hadn't even tried to contact Penny since she'd hung up on him so why did he feel like he was still doing something wrong? Making a monumental mistake of some kind?

'One other thing...' The chairman of the festival committee leaned closer to his microphone. 'We still haven't made a final decision about the charity that will be supported by the festival. If anyone has any more suggestions, they'll need to talk to a committee member tonight.'

Rafe found himself getting to his feet. Raising

his arm to signal one of the support crew who'd been providing microphones for the people who'd wanted to ask questions during the briefing.

'I have a suggestion,' he said, taking hold of the mike.

'And you are?'

'Rafe Edwards. My company is providing the fireworks to finish the festival.'

A ripple of interest turned heads in his direction. The chairman was nodding. 'You've made a significant contribution to the event,' he said. 'Thank you.'

The applause was unexpected. Unnecessary. Rafe cleared his throat. 'The message we've been hearing to tonight is that you want this to be a family-friendly event. A mini-festival that isn't a rave for teenagers but something that could become an annual celebration that will bring families together.'

'That's right.'

'So I have a suggestion for the charity that you might like to consider supporting.'

'Yes?'

'The Loxbury Children's Home—Rainbow House—is a facility that this town should be very proud of. It's changing the lives of the most vulnerable citizens we have—our disadvantaged children—and, with more funding and support, it could do even more good for the community.'

A murmur of approval came from the crowd and the chairman was nodding again, after exchanging glances with the other committee members on the stage.

'It's local,' the chairman said. 'And it's about family. It's certainly a good contender.' A nod signalled that the evening's agenda was complete. 'Thanks, everybody. You'll find some refreshments in the foyer. I look forward to seeing you all again on Saturday evening. And, Mr Edwards? Come and see me before you go. I'd like to provide some free passes for the children at Rainbow House to come to the festival.'

Rafe hadn't intended staying to drink tea or eat any of the cake the Loxbury Women's Institute was providing, but there seemed to be a lot of people who wanted to shake his hand and tell him how appreciated the contribution of his fireworks show was and what a good idea he'd had for the charity to be supported.

One of them was Paddy Murphy.

'Kids are everything, aren't they?' He smiled. 'They're the future. Biggest regret of my life was not having any of my own.'

Close up for the first time, there was no doubt in Rafe's mind that this man *was* Penny's father. Those liquid brown eyes were familiar enough to twist something in his chest. About where his heart was. But he had to return the friendly smile. Say something casual.

'I'll probably have the same regret one day.' Oops. That wasn't exactly casual, was it? He shrugged. 'It's a hard road, finding the right woman, I guess.'

'Oh, I found her.' The Irish brogue was as appealing as the sincerity in Paddy's gaze. 'But then I lost her.' He slapped Rafe on the shoulder and turned away but then looked back with a shake of his head. 'Truth be told, *that's* really the biggest regret of my life. Always will be.'

Rafe watched him disappear into the crowd.

And it was right about then that he realised why he couldn't shake that nagging feeling of making some huge mistake.

He knew what that mistake was.

He just didn't have any idea of how to fix it.

CHAPTER TEN

WHAT ON EARTH was she going to do with all
these cakes?

Chocolate and banana and carrot and red velvet. All iced and decorated and looking beautiful,
and Penelope had no desire to eat a bite of any
of them. The baking marathon had been therapy.
Something comforting to do while she tried to
sort through the emotional roller-coaster of the
last couple of days.

She could take one of them in to the hospital
for the lovely nurses who were caring for her
grandfather so well. Maggie and Dave were always happy to have a cake in the house and her
grandmother might like to take one home to help
Rita cater for the stream of well-wishers that
were turning up at their door. And maybe—the

thought came as a gleam of light at the end of a dark tunnel—she could take one to Rafe.

To say sorry. Of course it couldn't make things right again but…it would be something, wouldn't it?

An excuse to see him one last time, anyway.

She chose the chocolate cake for the nurses in the cardiology ward of Loxbury General.

'You didn't need to,' the nurse manager told her. 'It's been a pleasure, caring for your grandad. We'll be sorry to see him go home tomorrow. But thank you…we *love* cake.'

She gave her grandmother the choice of the other cakes.

'Could I take the red velvet? I know your Grandad loved his birthday cake and it *was* rather delicious.'

'Of course. I'm sorry—I didn't think to make a Madeira one.'

'Do you know, I think I'm over Madeira. Such a boring cake, when you come to think of it.'

There was no farewell hug or kiss after hand-ing over the cake but Penelope still felt good. There was something very different about her relationship with her grandmother now. Something that had the promise of getting better. Just like Grandad.

The smile stayed with her as she drove to Rainbow House. How good had it been to sit and hold Grandad's hand in the last few days? To talk to him about things they'd never discussed and even to tell him about that extraordinary conversation with her grandmother.

'She did do her best with you, you know. And she does love you, even if she doesn't let herself admit how much. She got broken by your mother's death, love. We both did. Nobody's perfect, you know. We all make mistakes but what really counts is who's there to hold your hand when it matters.'

'I know.' It was a poignant thought to realise whose hand she would want to be holding hers in a crisis.

Only she'd want more than that, wouldn't she?

She'd want her whole body to be held. So that she could feel the way she had when Rafe had held her.

'Loving people carries such a risk of getting hurt, doesn't it?' There had been an apology in her grandfather's voice as he'd patted her hand. 'Maybe neither of us was as brave as we should have been.'

Penelope's smile wobbled now as she turned into a very familiar street. How brave was she?

Brave enough to take one of those cakes to Rafe's office? To ask that receptionist if there was a chance that the terribly important chief executive officer of All Light on the Night might have the time to see her?

Not that he'd be at work this late in the day.

Maybe it would be better to take the cake to Loxbury Hall? To the place where she had fallen in love with him…

The place where he'd made *her* feel loved…

Phew… Just as well she had a visit to make to Rainbow House first. Some time with Maggie and Dave and the kids was exactly what she needed to centre herself before taking a risk like that.

How awful would it be if he didn't want to see her?

'Cake… And it's not even Sunday.' Maggie's hug was as warm as ever. 'Come in, hon. How's your grandad?'

'Going home tomorrow. His arteries are full of stents and probably better than they've been for a decade or more. Good grief, Maggie…what's that terrible noise?'

A naked, giggling toddler trotted past, with Dave in pursuit. 'I think we have you to thank for that racket.' He shook his head but he was grinning.

Charlene's hair was orange today. She went past with her fingers in her ears.

'I can't stand it,' she groaned. 'Someone tell him to stop.'

'Maggie?'

'Go and see for yourself. Out in the shed.' Maggie looked at the wet footprints on the hall floor. 'I'd better give Dave a hand with the baths.'

Bemused, Penelope put the cake in the kitchen and kept going through the back door to the old shed at the far end of the garden. The noise got steadily louder. A banging and crashing that had to be a set of drums, but they weren't being played by anyone who knew what they were doing.

Sure enough, opening the door and stepping cautiously into the cacophony, she saw it was Billy who was surrounded by the drum set. He was giving it everything he had—an expression of grim determination on his face. And then he stopped and the sudden silence was shocking.

'That was rubbish, wasn't it?'

Penelope opened her mouth to say something reassuring but someone else spoke first.

'Better than my first attempt.'

Rafe… She hadn't seen him in the corner of the dimly lit shed, sitting on a bale of the straw kept to line the bottom of the rabbit's hutch. Billy had his back to her but if Rafe had noticed her entrance he didn't show it. His attention was on the young boy he'd rescued from that imminent explosion.

'You're doing well all round, Billy. Maggie's told me how hard you're trying.'

Maybe she was interrupting something private. Penelope turned. The door was within easy reach. She could slip out as unobtrusively as she'd come in.

'I'm following the rules,' Billy said. 'Like Penny told me to. So that—you know—people'll like me.'

'Penny's an amazing lady,' Rafe said.

The tone of something like awe in his voice captured Penelope so instantly that there was no way she could make her feet move. Was it possible his feelings went further than merely being impressed by her? A smile tugged at her lips but then faded rapidly as Rafe kept talking.

'What she said, though…well, it's absolute rubbish, Billy.'

That stung. Without thinking, Penelope opened her mouth. 'How can you say that?'

Rafe must have seen her come in because he didn't seem nearly as surprised as Billy that she was there. The boy's head jerked around to face her but the shift in Rafe's gaze was calm.

'You've always followed all the rules,' he said. 'How's that worked out for you?'

'Just fine,' Penelope said tightly. What sort of example was Rafe giving Billy by saying this?

She glared at him. He had his cowboy hat on and the brim was shading his face but he was staring back at her just as intently. She could *feel* it.

'Sometimes you haven't followed all the rules. How's *that* working out?'

Oh…maybe he was providing a good example after all. What were those rules she'd broken? The only one she could think of right now was the time she'd gone upstairs at Loxbury Hall when she'd thought it was forbidden. When she'd given herself to Rafe.

She dropped her gaze to try and shield herself from the intensity of that scrutiny. 'Not so good.'

'You sure about that?' The quiet voice held a note of…good grief…*amusement*? As if he knew very well how well it had worked out.

Billy's foot went down on the pedal to thump the bass drum. 'I don't get it,' he growled. 'One minute you're telling me to follow the rules and then you say stuff about *you* guys breaking them. It doesn't make sense.'

Rafe leaned forward on his straw bale, his hands on his knees, giving Billy his full attention again.

'There are a lot of rules that are important to follow, Billy, but people will like you for *who* you are. You just have to show them who that really is and not hide behind stuff.'

'What kind of stuff?'

'Some people try to hide by being perfect and following all the rules.'

Penelope winced.

'And some people try to hide by making out they're tough and they don't care.'

Billy was twisting the drumsticks he still held. 'I *don't* care.'

'Yeah, you do.' The gentle note in Rafe's voice made Penelope catch her breath. 'We *all* care.'

'You don't know anything.' Billy's head was down. The drumsticks were very still.

'I know more than you think. I *was* you once, kid. I was tough. I didn't give a damn and I broke every rule I could and got into trouble all the time. And you know why?'

It took a long time for the reluctant word to emerge.

'Why?'

'Because I didn't *want* to care. Because it was too scary to care. Because that was how you got hurt.'

The long silence then gave the impression that Billy was giving the matter considerable thought but when he spoke he sounded offhand.

'Is it true we're all going to go and see the fireworks tomorrow night?'

Rafe didn't seem to mind the subject being changed. 'You bet.'

'You got us the tickets,' Billy said. He paused. 'And the drums.'

'The tickets are for everybody. The drums are just for you.'

'For real?'

'For real.' Rafe was smiling. 'And you know why I gave them to you?' He didn't wait for a response but he did lower his voice, as though the words were intended only for Billy. He must have known Penelope could hear, though. Without the drums, it was utterly quiet in there.

'Because I care. It's okay to care back, you know. It's quite safe.'

He got to his feet and took a step towards Penelope. But his words had been directed at Billy just then. Hadn't they? Her stupid heart skipped a beat anyway. A tingle of something as wonderful as hope filling a space around it that had been very empty.

Billy's sideways gaze was suspicious. 'Do you care about her, too?'

The brim of that hat made it impossible to read the expression in Rafe's eyes but she didn't need to. She could hear it in the sound of his voice.

'Oh, yeah…'

Billy made a disgusted sound. 'You gonna get married, then? And have kids?'

'Um… Bit soon to think about anything like that. And I might have to find out how Penny feels first, buddy.'

Billy's tone was accusing now. 'You care, too, don't you?'

Penelope couldn't drag her gaze away from Rafe. 'Oh, yeah…'

The delicious silence as the mutual declaration was absorbed finally got broken by a satisfied grunt from Billy that indicated the matter was settled. 'Can I go and tell the other kids that the drums are just for me?'

'How 'bout telling them that they're going to have the best time ever at the festival tomorrow? And tell Maggie and Dave that you'll help look after the little ones. Fireworks can be a bit scary close up and I'm going to make sure you have the very best place to watch.'

It was still hard to tell if his words were just for Billy or whether he was reminding Penelope of when he'd taken her to the best place to watch his fireworks.

Billy was on his feet now, though—his skinny chest puffed with pride. 'I can do that.' He put his drumsticks on the stool. 'I'm one of the biggest kids here.'

He had to walk between Rafe and Penelope to get to the door but neither of them seemed to notice because he was below the line of where they were looking—directly at each other.

His steps slowed. And then stopped. The suspense was getting unbearable. Rafe was going to kiss her the moment Billy disappeared and Penelope didn't want to have to wait a second longer.

But Billy turned back. He went back to the stool and picked up the drumsticks. 'I'm gonna need these.'

Rafe grinned. 'Practise on a cushion for a bit. That way you won't drive anyone crazy.'

'I think I might be going crazy,' Penelope murmured, as Billy disappeared through the door of the shed.

'Me, too.' Rafe pushed the door closed. 'Crazy with wanting you.'

But he didn't move any closer. They stood there, for the longest time, simply looking at each other.

'Me, too.' The words escaped Penelope on a sigh. 'I love you, Rafe...'

He held out his hand. Without saying a word, he led her over to the straw bale and sat down beside her. Then he took off his hat and held it in his hands.

Penelope swallowed hard. She'd said it first and he hadn't said it back. He hadn't uttered a single word since she'd spoken.

He could have kissed her instead. That would have been enough. But he hadn't done that either.

She was standing on a precipice here.

Teetering.

Feeling like she might be about to fall to her death.

She'd said she cared.

Not just the way you could care about a lost kid and want to do something to help put him on the right path, even though that kind of caring could be so strong you had to put yourself out there and maybe face stuff that you thought you'd buried a long time ago.

Penelope had gone further. She'd said she *loved* him. She'd just gone right out there and said the scariest thing in the world. Put herself in the place where you could hurt the most.

The weight of how that made him feel had crushed his ability to form words. To form coherent thoughts even, because what he said next could be the most important thing he ever said in his life.

No pressure there...

That weird weight seemed to be too much for his body as well as his brain. He had to sit down, but he wasn't going anywhere without Penny and she seemed happy enough to take his hand and follow along.

But now he had to say something. He heard the little hitch in her breath in the silence. A sound that made him all too aware of how scared she was.

He was scared, too. His hands tightened on his hat, scrunching the felt beneath his fingers.

'You know why I bought Loxbury Hall?' His voice sounded rusty.

From the corner of his eye, he saw Penelope nod. 'You told me. That night—in the bath. You said it was the kind of house that only people who had perfect lives could live in.'

'Yeah... That's what I thought through all those rough years when my life was like Billy's. If you were rich enough, you could make your own rules. Live in a place like that and have a family that stayed together. You called family a safe place once and I guess that's what a huge house that cost a bucket of money represented to me. That safe place. But you know what?'

Her voice was a whisper. 'What?'

'I was wrong. So, so wrong.' The whole hat was twisted in his hands now. It would never be the same. Dropping it, he turned his head to look at Penelope. His empty hands caught hers.

'The safe place isn't a place at all, is it? It's a person.'

Her eyes were huge. Locked on his, and it felt as if something invisible but solid was joining them.

'But it's a place, too. Not a place you can buy. Or even find a map of how to get there. It's the place that you're in when you're with *that* person.'

Her eyes were shining now. With unshed tears? Was he saying something that she understood? That she wanted to hear?

Even if she didn't, it felt right to say it. Maybe so that he could understand it better himself.

'It's a place that only that person can create with you. You can't see it but it's so real that even when you're not together you can still feel safe because you know where that place is.' He had to pause to draw in a slow, steadying breath.

This was it.

The thing he really had to say.

'You're my person, Penny.'

Yep. They had been unshed tears. They were escaping now.

Her voice was the softest whisper but he could hear it as clear as a bell and it felt just as good as if she were shouting it from a rooftop.

'You're my person, too, Rafe. For ever and always.'

CHAPTER ELEVEN

THE WEATHER GODS smiled on Loxbury for the thirtieth anniversary of their first music festival and the lazy, late-summer afternoon morphed into an evening cool enough for people to enjoy dancing but still warm enough for the ice-cream stalls to be doing a brisk business.

The gates had opened at five p.m. and the fireworks show timed for ten p.m. had been widely advertised as something people wouldn't want to miss—an exciting finale to a memorable occasion.

It was a music festival with a difference. Artists who'd been at the original festival were given star billing, of course, but there were many others. New local groups, soloists, dance troupes, a pipe band and even the entire Loxbury symphony orchestra. The appreciative crowd was just as eclectic a mix as the entertainment on offer. Teenagers were out in force, banding together far enough away from parents to be cool, but there were whole families there as well, staking out their picnic spots on the grass with blankets and folding chairs, prams and even wheelchairs.

Between the musical performers, the MC introduced the occasional speaker. At about eight p.m., when the crowd had swelled to record numbers, the person who came out to speak was the mayor of Loxbury, resplendent in his gown and chain.

'What a wonderful event this is,' he said proudly. 'A credit to the countless people who have given up so much of their time both to organise and perform. Thank you, all.'

The cheer that went up from the crowd expressed their appreciation.

'I came to the very first festival,' the mayor continued. 'And I remember how much opposition there was to it even happening. There was even a petition taken to the council to try and prevent it corrupting our young people.'

There was laughter from the crowd now. Penelope caught Maggie's glance and shared a smile. Rainbow House had several rugs on the grass. The younger children had all visited the face-painting booths and even Billy had been persuaded to have his face painted white with a black star around his eye to look like the lead singer of Kiss. Right now, he was sitting with the youngest children, righting the occasional ice-cream cone that threatened to lose its topping.

'I can't see any dangers here,' the mayor smiled. 'Just a heart-warming number of our families having a great time together.'

It was a poignant moment for Penelope. She'd never dreamed of attending such an event in her life because she'd grown up with the belief that terrible things did, in fact, happen at music festivals. She'd considered herself living proof of exactly that.

'I see parents and grandparents,' the mayor

continued. 'And I see many of our youngest citizens, who represent the future of Loxbury. Some of you know the story of Baby X—the baby that got found when they were cleaning up after that first festival that we're celebrating again today. That baby got returned to its family but we all know there are some children that aren't always that lucky, and it's my pleasure to tell you that the charity chosen to benefit from this festival is a place that cares for those children. Rainbow House…'

The clapping and cheering were deafening this time but Maggie burst into tears. Dave took her into his arms and Penelope suspected he shed a few tears as well. She had to blink hard herself because she knew what this could mean. The roof getting fixed, along with a dozen other much-needed repairs. All sorts of things that could make life more comfortable and enable these people she loved to keep doing something so wonderful. She might suggest a minibus so that they could transport the children more easily when they had somewhere special to go.

Like the festival today, which had presented a logistical challenge. And the Christmas party that was going to take place this year at Loxbury Hall. It had been a joy planning that with Rafe last night, and she knew it would happen. She was going to talk to Jack this week about the catering they would be doing for it.

The other crazy schemes they'd come up with might need some adjustment. Turning a wing of Loxbury Hall into offices so they could both work at home might be a waste because he'd still want to travel to his big shows. And she might want to go with him. Making the hall and gardens available as a wedding venue again needed thinking about, too. It was very likely to become their home and would they want to share that with strangers—especially when they had their own family to think about?

But how much happiness could it bring? Maggie and Dave had never hesitated to share their home and some of the people cheering so loudly right now were probably those teenagers who had come to find Maggie and Dave from amongst the gathering just to say hello. Young people who had needed shelter at some time in their lives and had a bond that would never fade. They seemed to be heading in this direction again to share the joy of this announcement and her bonus parents were going to be busy giving and receiving hugs for quite some time. She made sure hers was the first.

How lucky had she been to find that bond herself?

How lucky was Billy?

And something else made her feel that she could never become any luckier. After what Rafe had whispered in her ear last night, maybe the next wedding she was going to manage was going to be her own. That would certainly happen at Loxbury Hall. And there was her birthday in a couple of days. Not that she needed any gifts because she had everything she could possibly want in her life now, but a small party would be nice. One that could be an invitation for her grandparents to share her new life in a meaningful way?

The mayor had finished speaking and the MC was introducing one of Loxbury's newer talents. Penelope recognised the group instantly as Diversion—the band that had played at the Bingham wedding. Were Clarissa and Blake here somewhere? If they were, they were probably dancing with the growing number of people in front of the stage. It was starting to get darker and there were glow sticks in abundance as well as headbands that had glowing stars or flashing lights on them.

Billy was on his feet now, jiggling a little on the spot as he listened to the music with his whole body. Penelope could see his hands twitching as if he was holding imaginary drumsticks. But then he stopped to stare at the stage, his black lipstick making his open mouth rather comical.

'Is that...*Rafe*?'

The band was playing a cover of Billy Joel's 'Just the Way You Are'.

Penelope could only nod in response. She'd known that Rafe would be joining the band for this song. He'd told her about it last night, when they'd left the shed in the garden, excused themselves from sharing cake and had gone to the best place in the world to celebrate the declaration of their love—where it had first begun—at Loxbury Hall. The most magnificent place that wasn't as important as the place he'd found with her.

The tears were too close again now. He'd told her what song he was going to be playing. He'd whispered the words as if they'd been written for him to say and it was his voice she could hear now, rather than Diversion's lead singer as he sang that he would take her just the way she was. That he wanted her just the way she was. That he loved her just the way she was.

And each time these lyrics led to a saxophone riff from the black-clad figure in the cowboy hat that had Penelope's total attention. Every bend and sway of his body ignited an all-consuming desire that she knew would never fade. The words were exactly how she felt. This love would never fade either.

The jab of Billy's elbow prevented her from turning into a mushy puddle.

'What's that thing he's playing?'

'A saxophone. He started learning it after he stopped playing on those drums he gave you.'

'That's what I'm gonna do, too.'

'Good idea.' Penelope took a deep breath as the song finished. 'I'll see you later, Billy. I told Rafe I'd meet him after this song to see how it's going with setting up the fireworks.'

'Can I come, too?'

'You promised to help look after the little ones, remember? You're in the best place to watch and it's not that far away.'

It was just as well there was an acceptable excuse not to take Billy with her. The setting up of the fireworks had been finished by lunchtime today. She was meeting Rafe near the stage simply so that they could be together and she couldn't have kissed him like this if there'd been anyone around to watch.

Couldn't have been held so close and basked in the bliss of all those feelings she'd had during the song that were magnified a thousand times by being pressed against his body. Being able to touch him—and kiss him—just like this.

But Rafe wanted to do more than kiss her.

'Come and dance with me.'

'No-o-o...I can't dance.' Penelope could feel the colour rising in her cheeks. 'You know that. You *saw* me trying to dance in your maze...'

'Ah, but you weren't dancing with *me*...'

And there they were. Among a hundred people dancing in front of the stage to the music from an Irish band that had been announced as one of the original festival artists, and it *was* easy. All she had to do was follow Rafe's excellent lead. They danced through the entire set the band played and then they stood and clapped as the band members took their turns accepting the applause.

The lead guitarist leaned in to the microphone and held up his hand to signal a need for silence.

'It's been thirty years since we played here,' he said. 'But my heart has always been in Loxbury.'

He waited for the renewed applause to fade.

'The love of my life was a Loxbury girl.'

Rafe's hand tightened around Penelope's and she felt an odd stillness pressing in on her. She was still in a crowd but she felt as conspicuous as if a spotlight had been turned onto her. Alone.

No, not alone. She had Rafe by her side.

'Who is he?'

'His name's Paddy Murphy.'

'*Patrick* Murphy?'

'I came to that first Loxbury festival hoping to find her again but I didn't.' Paddy shook his head sadly. 'There's never been anyone else for me but that's just the way things worked out, I guess. Maybe you're out there tonight, Charlie, my darlin'. If you are, I hope you're happy. Here's one more song—just for you...'

People around started dancing again but

Penelope was standing as still as a stone. 'Oh, my God…' she whispered.

Rafe led her away from the dancers before anyone could bump into them. Right away from any people. He took them into the area fenced off as the safety margin for the pyrotechnic crew by showing his pass to a security guard. Off to the edge of field that was criss-crossed with wires leading to the scissor lifts.

'Watch your feet. Don't trip…'

The music was fainter now and the people far enough away to be forgotten. Except for one of them.

'He's my father, isn't he?'

'I think he probably is. He looks a lot like you, close up. And he's a really nice person. Special…'

'Did you know about him being here?'

'I knew his name and that his band was going to be playing. And then I met him a couple of nights ago and he told me that losing the woman he loved was the biggest regret of his life.' Rafe drew Penelope close to kiss her. 'That was the moment I realised that I'd be making the biggest mistake of my life if I lost you. That you were the love of *my* life.'

'He doesn't know about what happened to my mother, does he?'

'Apparently not.'

'You know what I think? I think that she brought me here to meet him. That he was the love of *her* life, too.'

'He told me something else, too. That his other huge regret was never having kids of his own.'

Penelope had a lump in her throat the size of a boulder. 'Do you think he'd want to meet me?'

'How could anyone not want to?' Rafe kissed her again. 'To be able to claim a connection to you would make him feel like the luckiest man on earth. No...make that the *second* luckiest man.'

Oh...the way Rafe was looking at her right now. Penelope wanted to be looked at like that for the rest of her life.

'I think I'd like to meet him,' she said softly. 'But it's pretty scary.'

'I'd be with you,' Rafe told her. 'Don't ever be scared. Hang on…'

The buzz of the radio clipped to his belt interrupted him and Penelope listened as he talked to his crew. The countdown to the fireworks was on. The orchestra was in position.

'This is a show to live music,' Rafe told her. 'It's a complicated set-up with manual firing.'

'Don't you need to be there?'

'That's what I train my crew to do. I'm exactly where I need to be.'

'And the orchestra's going to play it?'

'Along with the bagpipes. Can you hear them warming up?'

The drone of sound was getting louder. The lights set up around the field were suddenly shut down, plunging the whole festival into darkness. Glow sticks twinkled like coloured stars in a sea of people that knew something exciting was about to happen. Penelope and Rafe were standing behind the stage, between the main crowd and the firing area. Rafe turned Penelope to face the scissor lifts and stood behind her, holding her in his arms.

An enormous explosion sent a rocket soaring into the night sky and the rain of colour drew an audible cry from thousands of throats. And then the music started, the bagpipes backed up by the orchestra.

'Oh…' She knew this music. Everybody did.

'You'll Never Walk Alone'. An anthem of solidarity.

Penelope had never been this close to fireworks being fired before. The ground reverberated beneath her feet with every rocket. The shapes and colours were mind-blowingly beautiful but flaming shards of cardboard were drifting alarmingly close to where they were standing.

And yet Penelope had never felt safer.

Here, in Rafe's arms.

They would never walk alone. They had each other.

'Wait till you see the lancework at the very

end,' Rafe told her. 'It took us a long time to build.'

The intensity of the show built towards its climax. Blindingly colourful. Incredibly loud. How amazing was it to still hear the crowd at the same time? Surely every single person there had to be singing at the tops of their voices to achieve that.

Penelope wasn't singing. Neither was Rafe. She could feel the tension in his body as the final huge display began to fade and something on the highest scissor lift came to life.

The biggest red love heart ever. And inside that was a round shape with something square inside that. Chains and a crown on the top. It was a coin. An old-fashioned penny. It even had the words 'One Penny' curving under the top.

'For you,' Rafe whispered. 'For my Penny.'

It was too much. Something private but it was there for the whole world to see. Penny. The person she really was. The person she'd tried to hide until Rafe had come into her life. Her smile wobbled precariously.

'A penny's not worth much these days.'

'You couldn't be more wrong. My Penny's worth more than my life.'

Rafe turned her in his arms so that he could kiss her. Slowly. So tenderly she thought her heart might break, but it didn't matter if it did because she knew that Rafe would simply put the pieces back together again.

Every time.

* * * * *

MILLS & BOON®
Large Print – September 2015

THE SHEIKH'S SECRET BABIES
Lynne Graham

THE SINS OF SEBASTIAN REY-DEFOE
Kim Lawrence

AT HER BOSS'S PLEASURE
Cathy Williams

CAPTIVE OF KADAR
Trish Morey

THE MARAKAIOS MARRIAGE
Kate Hewitt

CRAVING HER ENEMY'S TOUCH
Rachael Thomas

THE GREEK'S PREGNANT BRIDE
Michelle Smart

THE PREGNANCY SECRET
Cara Colter

A BRIDE FOR THE RUNAWAY GROOM
Scarlet Wilson

THE WEDDING PLANNER AND THE CEO
Alison Roberts

BOUND BY A BABY BUMP
Ellie Darkins

MILLS & BOON®
Large Print – October 2015

THE BRIDE FONSECA NEEDS
Abby Green

SHEIKH'S FORBIDDEN CONQUEST
Chantelle Shaw

PROTECTING THE DESERT HEIR
Caitlin Crews

SEDUCED INTO THE GREEK'S WORLD
Dani Collins

TEMPTED BY HER BILLIONAIRE BOSS
Jennifer Hayward

**MARRIED FOR THE
PRINCE'S CONVENIENCE**
Maya Blake

THE SICILIAN'S SURPRISE WIFE
Tara Pammi

HIS UNEXPECTED BABY BOMBSHELL
Soraya Lane

FALLING FOR THE BRIDESMAID
Sophie Pembroke

A MILLIONAIRE FOR CINDERELLA
Barbara Wallace

FROM PARADISE...TO PREGNANT!
Kandy Shepherd

MILLS & BOON®

Why shop at millsandboon.co.uk?

Each year, thousands of romance readers find their perfect read at millsandboon.co.uk. That's because we're passionate about bringing you the very best romantic fiction. Here are some of the advantages of shopping at www.millsandboon.co.uk:

* **Get new books first**—you'll be able to buy your favourite books one month before they hit the shops

* **Get exclusive discounts**—you'll also be able to buy our specially created monthly collections, with up to 50% off the RRP

* **Find your favourite authors**—latest news, interviews and new releases for all your favourite authors and series on our website, plus ideas for what to try next

* **Join in**—once you've bought your favourite books, don't forget to register with us to rate, review and join in the discussions

Visit **www.millsandboon.co.uk**
for all this and more today!